35¢

ROCKETS
IN URSA MAJOR

1817

HARPER & ROW, PUBLISHERS,

based on the play of that title

by Fred Hoyle

ROCKETS
IN URSA MAJOR

a novel by

FRED HOYLE and

GEOFFREY HOYLE

NEW YORK AND EVANSTON

To BARBARA, BERNARD
and JOSEPHINE

ROCKETS
IN URSA MAJOR

PROLOGUE

The sun beat mercilessly down on the concrete launching pads at Mildenhall. The DSP 15 stood alone, glinting in the light of high noon. The apron around the ship was a hive of activity as the countdown drew to a close.

'Best of luck, Fanshawe,' said John Fielding, the scientific leader of the project. 'When you return I shall have aged much more than you.'

'If your bally refrigerator works properly, Fielding,' replied the ship's Commander. 'I can't quite see myself doing a recce in Ursa Major with a crew of abominable Snowmen.' He turned to his crew. 'Right-ho, chaps, off we go. I'll tuck you up in the ice-box when we're on course.'

He held out his hand to Fielding. 'Don't look so worried. We really have absolute faith in the whole machine, so you'd better start looking to that jolly old beacon of yours, and make lots of toddy when you get our re-entry signals. We shall need it.' John Fielding smiled and they shook hands.

Tubby Fanshawe moved towards the lift. Suddenly he stopped, and looked hard at a young blushing red-haired space cadet. 'Ganges! 'Pon my soul, what's the

1

Space Corps coming to? You must have concealed your batting averages.'

'Good luck, Fanshawe. I'm not supposed to be here, but couldn't resist seeing you off.' The young man beamed with pleasure at being recognized in the crowd.

'All the best to you, laddie,' said Fanshawe. 'Don't let the Generals grind you down.' With a last wave to the small crowd that had gathered, he climbed into the lift and was whisked to the crew's cabin at the nose of the ship.

Fifteen minutes later the rocket rose in a cloud of oxygen gas, exhaust flames and concrete dust, slowly tilting on its course for Ursa Major, and a page in history.

1

I'm not a great one for scientific conferences. This one had been particularly time-wasting, but as the plane left the ground the boredom of the last few days vanished. I settled back thankfully to think of more important problems.

'Hello, Dick,' came an American voice. I turned round to see Dave Swan Vespa, one of the top news reporters for N.B.C. International Television Company.

'How's your research project going?' he inquired.

'Too slowly,' I replied grumpily.

'Haven't you fellows got it working yet?' Dave grinned broadly. I grinned back and said nothing.

'See you soon, then.'

He moved off down the gangway. Dave's remark stirred up my irritation at the slow progress on the International radio transmitter. The idea was a good one. Started two years ago by the International Space Exploration Committee, it came after thirty years of almost total inactivity. Loss of exploratory ships in the early 1980s had led to a halt in deep space probes. The only work with space ships nowadays was in the defence of our planet and its environment. Now new life had been injected into space research with the building of this gigantic radio transmitter. Messages would be sent deep into space in the hope that someone somewhere would pick up our signals and transmit an answer back. My part in all this research was to develop a new form of radar valve. The whole programme was being almost defeated by insufficient money from disinterested governments. Despite this handicap the scientists kept their research work going as best they could.

When we landed, the usual English weather prevailed, which gave the airport an almost forlorn look in comparison with the bright sunlight of Los Angeles. I went by tube to the Hampstead Heliport, where I was just in time to catch the helicopter taxi to Cambridge.

I climbed in beside the driver. He picked up his punch cards, and selecting the Cambridge one pushed it into the reader. This meant information was fed to the central transport computer which would work out the best possible route, height and speed for the journey. All this information would then be passed to our destination so that, once we were in the air, automatic homing devices would take over and whisk us to our destination without traffic jams or accidents. The police have their own link-up with this comptuer. It greatly helps in crime detection, but I feel it is an infringement of individual liberty.

A few seconds later a green light appeared on the control panel. The driver fired up the small rocket motors and we lifted into the air, rising vertically until picked up by the homing frequency. The great advan-

4

tage of the jet against the conventional motor is the smoothness it offers as well as a slight increase in reliability.

It was a clear night, with the stars getting brighter the higher we went. With a light jolt the helicopter stopped rising and moved off in a forward direction.

All was quiet at the Cambridge terminal. My watch showed eleven in the morning. I turned it back eight hours, the time difference between California and London. It was now 3 a.m.

Dawn was starting to come up as I reached the rear gates of St John's College and inserted the old-fashioned key in the lock. The college authorities still hadn't turned over to the new computerized key systems. The metal tumblers clicked away, and I pushed the heavy wrought iron gates open. Locking them behind me, I made my way to my rooms.

When I opened the door, a strong smell of polish and fresh air hit me; my bedmaker had obviously had a spring clean while I'd been away. I walked to my desk, just to make sure that my papers were still there, and not in the waste basket, but they were safe. My travelling had made me hungry, so I descended to the kitchenette. Taking a packet of dehydrated eggs and bacon, I made myself a delicious pan of food. Back in the living-room, I flicked through the television channels until I found a good old film about the Wild West of America in the eighteen-thirties, and settled down before the screen, but the covered wagons and Indians

5

suddenly vanished and the newscaster's face appeared on the screen:

'We interrupt our programme with an important announcement from World Space Headquarters. The space ship DSP 15 has been picked up on its way back to Earth. Older viewers will recall that, almost thirty years ago to the day, this ship was sent out on a mission to the stars of the Ursa Major stream. . . . We have more important news about the DSP 15: it's going to land here in Britain! Stand by for further announcements, and now back to our film.'

The film continued, but I was no longer interested. For a moment the news stunned me. Then the phone went. I rushed over to the desk and flicked the switch. A small TV screen on the wall flickered and the picture and sound came.

It was Ganges, a high-ranking officer at the space drome at Mildenhall, a few miles to the east of Cambridge.

'Thank God you're back,' he said, before I could speak.

'Have you heard the news?'

'Yes, just. What on earth do you make of it?'

'I daren't think. . . . It's going to land here . . . and soon. . . .' Then Ganges' urgency turned to irony. 'That damned military computer can't find the coding instructions for opening it up.'

'You mean they're mislaid?' I said in disbelief.

'That's about it,' Ganges said candidly. His harassed voice continued, 'Can't get through to Sir John. It's im-

6

perative we contact him. He may have the files and we need him here.'

'All right. I'll go now. How long before you expect it?'

'An hour or so . . .' Ganges was about to add to this, but I just nodded as I switched him off.

I hurried out of my rooms and quickly descended the old stone staircase and out into the court. It wasn't far to where Sir John Fielding lived in a lovely old mill-house on the river. He'd resisted all persuasion from the local housing authorities and Senate House committee of the University to move. They wanted the house as a museum.

A sharp walk along the river bank brought me to Sir John's. I trod firmly on the door mat. A bell rang somewhere inside. Nothing happened, so I pressed urgently again. After a few minutes of standing with mounting impatience in the early morning half-light, I heard the latch click and the door swung in. With immense relief I saw it was Sir John.

'I'm sorry to get you out of bed, Sir John,' I began rather stupidly.

'Why do it?' he said sleepily.

'The DSP 15 is coming into Mildenhall. . . .'

The sleepy eyes opened wide. He was instantly alert. 'Come in.' He led me quickly into his study.

'This is quite fantastic, quite fantastic,' said Sir John, looking shaken. 'Coming in!'

'Yes, in about an hour. Ganges rang me up. They're

7

in great trouble. They have no landing instructions. I think Ganges was wondering . . .'

'What, Dick, what? That I might remember the code? Good God. What sort of memory do they think I've got—an elephant's? I don't even know where to start looking,' Sir John exploded, getting up and going over to his old filing cabinets. 'Let's get on with it.'

'Try that cabinet there,' he said briskly. 'I'll take this one. Red and green files all marked DSP 15/UM.'

It was nerve-racking trying not to panic. The papers were endless and not in order. Time was so short but I dared not think about it. Sir John was calmly, methodically thumbing through filing drawers, but his face was a grey mask of anxiety. Then unbelievably I found files marked DSP 15/UM. I gave them to Sir John.

'Are these the ones?'

He took them quietly. 'Good, good,' he said, quickly shuffling through them. 'Yes, these are they; not that one; that's injector system, this one's reactor details. Hmm. Interesting. Ah! here we are, carrier frequencies-pulse lengths 39.37 megacycles. This is it. We'll have the ship down safely and the crew out in a trice.' Sir John beamed happily.

'Come and talk to me while I quickly put some clothes on.'

While he was hurriedly dressing I asked him: 'Why 39.37 megacycles?'

'Number of inches in a metre,' he replied. 'Sort of technical joke, forgotten the point of it now.'

I let it pass. 'What equipment will you need?'

'Nothing unusual. Amplitude modulation, frequency modulation, pulsing and so forth, all straightforward stuff.'

He finished dressing and was off downstairs at a speed which astonished me. When I reached the hall he was nowhere to be seen, but noises led me to the kitchen. He had a Thermos flask ready, a kettle about to boil and was stirring an amber fluid with sugar in a glass jug. Nearby was a sliced lemon.

'What on earth is that?' I asked.

'Hot toddy,' he twinkled.

2

'All ready,' he said, filling the Thermos.

'Why is it coming into Mildenhall?' I asked, tightly holding on to the bundles of files.

'Oh, it's a long story. The ships fly on automatic pilot along a radio beam sent out from Earth. They have to, because the crew is all tucked away in the deep freeze containers to prevent serious ageing during long journeys.'

We moved out of the house. 'Well, when the ships didn't come back,' Sir John continued, 'and we'd completely lost contact with them, some people at headquarters thought there was little point in continuing the radio beams. The British representative fortunately didn't agree, and there was an argument about it. The result was that we here in Britain were given the job of maintaining the beams. Everyone else said it was a hopeless task, but it doesn't look that way now.'

I nodded, remembering the special building at Mildenhall for the beams. I'd done some work there when I was a student and had been told about them.

We walked on to the patio where a small helicopter stood, given to Sir John by one of the large aviation companies.

'Do you mind driving? I want to look at these,' Sir John said. He became deeply engrossed in the contents of one of the files as we took off.

On the outskirts of Cambridge there were a couple of police patrol helicopters. As we approached them our air speed began to reduce.

'What's wrong?' my companion asked, looking up from his work.

The police had obviously been told to stop us as they were indicating that I should take the helicopter down to the ground.

'What do you want?' shouted Sir John from his side of the helicopter. The police went on signalling us to descend.

'We've no option,' I said, taking the helicopter down.

'Damned idiots. We're in a hurry.' Sir John was beginning to get annoyed.

Down on the ground the police turned on powerful arc lights.

'All right, gentlemen. Why are you going to Mildenhall?' said one of the men in a challenging voice, leaning in through my side.

'They need me,' said Sir John crossly.

'And who might you be?' said the officer.

'This is Sir John Fielding. One of the original designers of the DSP 15 which is coming in to land at Mildenhall.'

'He may be, but you've got no clearance from Mildenhall.' The officer shrugged his shoulders. 'No luck, gentlemen.'

'I suggest you call Colonel Ganges at Mildenhall before you ground us, officer,' said Sir John in a cold even voice. 'And for God's sake, hurry!'

'Colonel Ganges. Eh! We'll see,' said the officer, trying to be sure of himself, but not quite knowing what to do. 'Get a Colonel Ganges at Mildenhall, will you?' he said to one of his men.

Sir John sat silently simmering, ready to explode.

'That's typical of Ganges,' Sir John said suddenly. 'He's so good at cutting red tape he's forgotten his own security arrangements and barred the only men who can help him.' Sir John smiled and leaned out of the window. He was about to say something when one of the policemen called:

'Colonel Ganges, sir.'

'Colonel Ganges. This is Sergeant Richards, Cambridge City Police. I've got a Sir John Fielding, a . . .' His sentence was cut short. 'But Colonel . . .' He tried to get a word in edgeways. Finally he handed the radio mike back. 'I must apologize, Sir John,' said the man.

'Quite all right, officer. Quite all right. It's not your fault.'

'Thank you, sir. We'll escort you to the space drome.'

'Good,' Sir John said briskly, and off we went.

Now, with top priority, we went at breath-taking speed.

A mile or two before we reached the space drome I could see a monumental amount of air activity. Our police escort started to hedge-hop, so down I went and followed them. Obviously all the official flight paths had gone to the military. Suddenly the police put down on the ground and I followed suit.

'It's absolute bedlam farther in,' the officer said, coming up to Sir John's window. 'Is there anything we can do?'

'Yes, just see that we get to Colonel Ganges as quickly as possible,' Sir John said, closing the file and climbing out.

We started hurrying across the field.

'There it is,' Sir John suddenly said, pointing to a shining needle sitting on the landing pad about a quarter of a mile away. It looked very small and thin in comparison with the large military ships dotted around the space drome. We stood in silence for a moment or two. I could feel Sir John's excitement. It was thirty years since he had last seen this ship, and it had been given up for lost by nearly everyone. Then he set off at a cracking pace across the acres of concrete. I almost had to run to keep up until he halted at the military cordon.

'Sir John Fielding and party,' said Sir John.

'Just one moment,' said the M.P. 'Sarge,' the M.P. yelled over his shoulder. 'A Sir John Fielding and party.'

The sergeant came over. 'Sir John,' he said, looking down a long list. 'Yes, here we are.'

'Dr Richard Warboys,' Sir John said, pointing at me.

'Dr Warboys, yes,' said the sergeant, ticking his list, and beckoning us through without looking up.

Near the rocket stood Ganges and some medics.

'Ah, Sir John,' said Ganges, uneasily. 'Sorry about the nonsense with the police. My stupid secretary. Silly fellow.'

'Damn your security and your filing system,' Sir John said, but without much heat. One of the medics came over.

'I'd like to get those men out as soon as possible, Sir John,' he said.

'I understand,' said Sir John quietly. 'Just give me a few minutes, a few minutes.'

'Can't see it matters to a few hours. Been frozen for donkey's years,' said Ganges in his usual bluff, tactless way.

'Of course it matters, Colonel,' said the doctor angrily. 'If we don't get in there very soon, those men are as good as dead. The shock of landing on hard frozen living material can be extremely severe.' The doctor was very agitated. Ganges on the other hand looked amazed at the doctor's outburst.

'Matter of urgency,' said Ganges, a little bleakly. 'Knew Tubby Fanshawe well. At school together.'

'Fanshawe,' said the doctor in surprise.

'Chief Pilot, doctor,' said Ganges, pointing a large porky finger at the ship. 'In there. Great spin bowler. Leg breaks and googlies.' Ganges then screwed himself up into a distorted version of a spin bowler's action. I had to smile, but I knew this fooling was Ganges way of hiding his true feelings.

An army engineer appeared out of a large radio hover

truck, walked over to us, saluted smartly and said: 'I'm afraid we can't do anything, Doc.'

'Colonel Ganges, this is quite intolerable. I can't be responsible for the lives of those men in there,' the doctor said.

'Dick,' Sir John said quickly. 'I've got it now.'

'What's that, Sir John?' said Ganges.

'We're just going to open the doors,' Sir John said, making his way over to the radio truck.

As I walked to the truck, I heard Ganges say: 'Doors need opening. Boffins. Amazin' fellas!' He followed us to the truck and looked in at the engineers and myself. 'Would you like help?'

'I think we'll make it,' I said, understanding how he felt.

Sir John nodded his agreement. Ganges still poked his head over Sir John's shoulder hesitantly and would probably have persisted but someone told him television reporters had got through the military cordon and he was off like a shot. God help them, I thought.

'First,' said Sir John's voice bringing me back to the problem in hand. 'I want a carrier at 174 megacycles. Then pulse it at 1 kc. pulse length 5 micro-seconds.'

'Carrier at 174 megacycles,' I said, moving a small dial.

'Pulse 1 kc. length 5 micro-seconds.' I changed over to another circuit. A pulse came and settled down, allowing me to set the pulse length at 5 micro-seconds.

'All right,' I said to an engineer standing close by. 'Just check everything for me.'

The man ran through the check list.

'Secondly,' Sir John said when the engineer signalled that everything was satisfactory, 'I want a separate transmission on 39.37 megacycles frequency modulated, amplitude 5 decibels below the first transmission.'

'Frequency modulation,' I blurted aloud. Sir John looked a bit irritated.

'We've still to key in the final numerical combination. This is done on the frequency modulation.'

I would have queried this type of operation, but there were more important things to do. 'Have you a key?' I asked one of the engineers.

'No, but we'll fix one up in a moment or two, sir,' said the poor engineer, who was obviously terrified of making a mistake.

'Check frequency,' I said, turning back to the dials in front of me.

'O.K.,' came the reply.

'Amplitude ratio?'

'O.K.'

'Key plugged in?'

'All ready, sir.'

'Right, Sir John. What's the code number?' I said, trying to emulate his steadiness. More than thirty years had elapsed since the crew in the rocket had left the earth, now we were on the threshold of seeing and hearing what they had seen and done.

'137131929,' said Sir John in triumph.

'What system?' I asked.

'Old fashioned Morse.'

17

'137131929 in old fashioned Morse,' I said to the engineer. He looked aghast for a moment and then went to work. I tried to look encouraging.

The engineer worked on. I could see beads of sweat on his forehead. My hands felt damp, as I listened to the sound of the digits being keyed in. 1 . . . 3 . . . 7 . . . 1 . . . 3 . . . 1 . . . 9 . . . 2 . . . 9. Then silence. It was almost agony waiting. Everyone must have been thinking the same thought. What happens if the systems jammed or something was damaged after such a long flight? We waited.

Then, as we held our breath, there was a satisfying click and deep rumble. I went to the door of the truck and stood with Sir John watching. The large doors up on the ship slowly began to open. We had succeeded. I felt Sir John relax. The strain for him must have been quite enormous; for even I felt drained of physical energy.

Two of the ground staff climbed on board a lift and drove it over to the side of the ship. For a moment or two they remained at the bottom, and then they pressed the button and went up. They vanished inside. Soon one of them returned to the doors of the rocket and signalled.

The medics were the first to the lift, with Ganges, Sir John and myself a long way behind.

'Remember Tubby Fanshawe scoring a cracking good 50—school cricket, if you know what I mean. Now frozen solid. Damn' amazing!' said Ganges, waiting impatiently for the lift to return.

The lift came down slowly. As we went up I realized how small this ship really was. The main doors, which were very near the top of the craft, would only come about half-way up one of the machines standing close by.

Amazing, I thought to myself, as we passed in through the doors, no airlock, and there would be no gravitational field inside the ship as we had today. The passage from the opening led straight into the cabin, the only cabin, which was used for everything, and in one half of the cabin was the freezer. A sort of cylinder-shaped cubicle with a large deep-freeze-type door. I left everyone to get on with opening it up and had a quick look round the rest of the cabin. A long console seemed to house most of the equipment. A museum-piece computer punch card machine, hand stabilizing equipment for adjusting the flight of the ship. It was a remarkable feat, to go out to Ursa Major with a small ship like this. Even my lab in Cambridge was better equipped, I thought, picking up a small drill.

'There's something seriously wrong,' I suddenly heard the doctor saying.

'What?' Sir John asked anxiously.

'The temperature is much too high.'

I went over to where the doctor and his medics stood. Ganges followed me over.

'Look at this, Sir John,' said the doctor, indicating the temperature gauge.

'What does the freezer normally operate at?' asked

Sir John, tapping the instrument like a barometer on the wall.

'Nowadays we'd operate at about −50° centigrade. I don't know precisely what the practice was thirty years ago, but it couldn't have been much different,' said the doctor, thoughtfully.

Sir John studied the dial. 'This gauge shows a temperature of about zero,' he said.

'Exactly, it's at thawing temperature.'

Curiosity got the better of me and I looked over a number of shoulders at the dial. It did indeed show a temperature of zero. 'Perhaps the automatic defrosters have worked,' I said.

'We can soon check on that,' said Sir John, moving, file in hand, over to the main control panel. 'You're right, Dick. That's what has happened,' he said, making his way back to the group.

We all stood in silence.

'I'm afraid the men's fate is pretty clear,' the doctor said, after a minute.

'Dead,' said Sir John quietly.

'I'm afraid so. Otherwise they'd have woken up by now. I'll have a look inside.' He started to open the large freezer door.

'This isn't my line of country. If you don't mind, I'll withdraw.'

'That would be best, Sir John. It won't be a pleasant job.'

Sir John and I moved away, followed by Ganges, who looked desperately glum. One could feel what he was thinking. It is never pleasant to learn that an old school pal has died. The medics were having a job to get the door open. A morbid thought crossed my mind. How long had the freezing chamber been thawed?

Sir John gently placed his Thermos on the control desk. He looked spent.

After much effort the heavy door swung open and the doctor went in. There was a moment's quiet and then he suddenly reappeared at the door. 'Hey. Just a minute, come and have a look in here.'

Ganges was the first across, followed closely by Sir John. I was a little hesitant, but followed them in, curiosity getting the better of me again. It reminded me of a mortuary in a hospital. Bleak, bare and cold, even though the temperature was above freezing. We went to the point where the crew should be in their containers.

'Great heavens, it's empty!' Sir John said, lifting one of the lids.

I opened another one and it was also empty; in fact so were they all.

'I don't understand,' I said. 'How could the ship have been started back to earth without a crew?'

'An interesting question,' Ganges said, squeezing his way out of the freezer. 'There must be a log-book somewhere.'

Sir John moved to a cabinet near the entrance and pulled open the drawers. 'That's very strange.'

'Nothing at all,' said Ganges, coming back to the middle of the cabin.

'This is ridiculous. The cabinet should be full of

ship's data like this,' Sir John said, waving the files he was carrying.

The problem of a ship with no crew and no papers was staggering. We all stood for a moment looking about not quite knowing what to do.

I moved round the cabin. Looking for what, I wasn't sure. I pressed the button on a tape manual deck. Nothing but high level static. Turning it off, I wondered how long it would take to sift through the information on the computer.

'Anything on the tape?' Sir John said, joining me.

'Nothing, just static.'

Sir John frowned, deep in thought. I felt at a loss.

'What would the crew be doing with a drill like this?' I asked Sir John, holding up the tool I had been playing with earlier.

'It looks like part of the doctor's equipment,' Sir John said.

'They carried a doctor with them?' said Ganges.

'Oh, yes. The drill looks like a dentist's drill.'

'So it can cut through fairly hard material?'

'I suppose so, but what are you driving at?'

Taking the drill from Sir John, I showed him the cutting edge. 'I thought it might have been used to cut a message on the metal.' I started moving my hand over all metal surfaces. The others did the same.

It took me about five minutes to find it. The maddening thing was that the engraving was right under where I'd found the instrument.

'I think this is what we've been looking for.'

22

I took my pen and scratched it over the markings.

'That's Fanshawe's signature,' said Sir John. 'Ganges, come here a moment.'

Ganges was already looking over Sir John's shoulder.

'Can you remember what Fanshawe's signature looked like?' I said.

'I think I can,' said Ganges peering hard. 'Yes, that's it. What was he doing?'

I went on covering the area with the black ink. We all read the message at the same time. I don't know what their reaction was, but I certainly felt very strange.

If this ship returns to Earth, then mankind is in deadly peril—God help you—

Fanshawe.

3

It was a macabre situation. No one offered a comment. It was too unreal, uncanny, spine chilling.

The doctor was the first to move.

'If I'm wanted I'll be over at control,' he said as he led his men out of the cabin.

Ganges waited for them to go. 'Can't make it out. What kind of situation could Tubby Fanshawe have got into?'

'Whatever it was, it's serious and sinister,' Sir John said sombrely.

We all made our way to the lift. Below were a large number of people.

'Ruddy press,' Ganges mumbled under his breath.

I wondered how he would handle the battery of TV cameras and reporters.

The lift came to a halt. The men and women in front of us moved forward. Military police advanced to clear a path.

'Colonel Ganges. Have you a comment?' said a man holding a microphone close to us.

'Yes,' Ganges replied. 'Get yourself and your gear back to the main building and wait for a press announcement. Sergeant Major?'

'Sir.'

'Cordon off this ship—top security. Report to me if any of the press crosses the boundary and I'll do the rest.'

The crowd parted and allowed us through. Everyone was subdued.

'I'll get on to the Minister of Defence, and see what kind of press release we'll put out,' Ganges said and moved in the direction of the control building. 'I'll be in touch.'

Sir John and I walked off towards the helicopter. Running footsteps behind us made him increase his pace.

'Sir John, was there something wrong with the ship's equipment?' came a voice from alongside us.

'As you heard, you'll have to wait until there's an official press release,' Sir John said, turning on his questioner.

'But Sir John, if it wasn't the equipment, how did the men die?'

Flash bulbs popped. Sir John turned on his heel. The press men followed us. I caught hold of the reporter who'd been asking questions. We stopped, allowing Sir John to get to the helicopter.

Before I could speak the M.P.'s were around us and the reporter moved for an uncomfortable interview with Ganges.

I climbed into the helicopter.

'Thank you, Dick. It could be very tricky if they found out that the ship's empty.'

'Well, Ganges knows his job and they won't be told

anything they're not supposed to know.' I slotted the card into the reader. The green light came on and off we went.

After a very quiet ride back, the helicopter started to home in on Sir John's residence. I kept the blip in the middle of the scope and we were soon down.

'Is there anything I can do?'

'No, not yet,' Sir John said with a tired smile. 'I'll give you a call if anything comes up.'

'Fine. I'll just stroll back to college; it looks as though it might be a fine morning.'

'Hum. By the way, if you should get any press . . .'

'Don't worry. I don't know anything,' I said, and made my way to the side entrance.

The summer mist was lying lightly on the river, and the early sun was catching the massive exteriors of the colleges. It was a strange discord that on such a beautiful morning there should be the nightmare aspect of the DSP 15 weighing heavily on our minds. My watch showed 08.15; breakfast in Hall wouldn't be until 08.30. I decided I'd go back to my rooms until around 09.00; by that time most of the college would have had their meal, I'd be able to have mine in peace.

But when I opened the door to my room, the phone was buzzing away imperiously.

'Hello, Dick,' said Sir John. 'The Minister of Defence has called an emergency meeting for ten-thirty this morning. I told the secretary that I would like to bring you along and he agreed. I'm off now to get one or two preliminaries worked out.'

'Fine. I'll be there, but why do you want me?'

'I think they'll be wanting your radar valve.'

'My valve, but it's only in the experimental stage?'

'Certainly, but time may be pressing. So be at the Ministry of Defence at 10.30 a.m.'

'O.K. Where do I go when I get there?'

'Room two,' said Sir John, vanishing from the screen.

Why on earth might they need my valve? What was to be gained at this stage by its use in a radio or radar system? I made myself a cup of coffee and went over to my desk. A few minutes of rummaging through one of the drawers and I found the necessary data. Putting it into my brief-case, I looked up the list of the helicopter services running from Cambridge to London. Once every quarter of an hour, which meant I could either catch the 09.30 or, at a pinch, the 09.45.

A shower, shave and change of clothes made me feel better. By the time I'd finished I was running late. The gate at the Heliport for the 09.30 to London was closed, but I caught the 09.45 and arrived at the Hampstead terminal around 10.15. I rushed out of the arrival building to find a taxi.

'If you're waiting for a taxi, I don't think you'll have much luck as I've been here fifteen minutes,' said a man sitting dejectedly at the head of the taxi queue.

'Thanks,' I said, going back into the building and making my way to the Underground.

The Houses of Parliament and Westminster Abbey stood gracefully surrounded by the greenery of a large park which had replaced the old buildings, such as Scotland Yard and other government offices. Alongside the ancient shining cannons little concrete bunkers were in evidence. These were the mammoth outlets for the air conditioning units under the ground.

I walked to the war monument in the middle of Whitehall. A couple of security guards stood outside.

'Yes, sir?' said one of the large fellows.

'Dr Warboys. I have a meeting with the Minister of Defence at 10.30,' I said.

'Running late,' the guard smiled as he checked a list. 'Dr Warboys. Fine.'

He opened a door and I stepped into the lift. It went down and down into a huge rabbit warren of government offices. Across the central hall another lift led straight into a vast conference room. Sitting at a large oval table were the Minister of Defence, the Chief of Staff and Sir John, with others I didn't recognize. The Chief of Staff was doodling away and Sir John was watching him as I stepped in.

'Ah, Dick,' said Sir John, getting up from the table and coming over to me. Under the briskness he still looked strained.

'Sorry I'm late,' I said contritely.

'It's all right, I told Lomax that you would be your usual punctual self. Minister, may I introduce Dr Richard Warboys,' said Sir John, addressing Sir Henry Lomax, the Minister of Defence.

'Good morning, Dr Warboys,' said the Minister curtly.

I sat down next to Sir John and acknowledged the

head noddings of the other men sitting at the table.

'Gentlemen. In view of the potential gravity of the situation, I thought it advisable to keep our meeting small in number,' said the Minister.

Everyone agreed.

'I think we should decide this morning on a plan of action which can then be passed on to World Space Headquarters. John,' said the Minister, turning in our direction, 'has any of the equipment in the DSP 15 been checked?'

'In what sense?' asked Sir John.

'Was it all functioning properly?' said the Minister.

'Well, we've run some preliminary tests and checked them against original data files. There's certainly nothing missing in the sense of components.'

The Chief of Staff suddenly looked up from his doodling and said: 'Well?'

'Well, until we have had time to run exhaustive tests, I can't be absolutely certain about a couple of points.'

'What do you mean?' said the Minister.

'Just strange little things. The computer will not operate on a simple test problem, and also there's nothing missing that could conceivably have been used to fire the rocket from outside.'

'I don't understand the problem with the computer. Surely it could have been damaged?' said the Chief of Staff.

'No, it looks more as if someone had wiped all the memories clean,' said Sir John.

'Hm. But getting back to the fact that there is no

missing equipment. You mean that the crew didn't abandon ship?' said the Minister of Defence.

'No, the crew didn't abandon ship,' said Sir John quickly.

'Unless they left it after the last firing, when it was automatically locked on a homeward course,' the doodler said.

'Yes. That's a possibility, but think of the problems,' Sir John replied.

'I agree, Sir John. But it is a possibility,' said the Chief of Staff.

'But I don't take that argument very seriously, Bob,' said the Minister to the Chief of Staff. Then he turned to Sir John. 'Just how do you reconstruct what might have happened?'

'I think the crew must have been taken forcibly from the ship, which was then deliberately set on its homeward course.'

'How?' said the Minister.

'By radio signals from outside,' said Sir John.

'From what equipment?' asked the Chief of Staff.

'It could have been equipment possessed by an alien intelligence,' said Sir John.

There was a stir around the table.

'Hm. An alien intelligence,' said the Minister. 'What would you say to that, Bob?' turning to the Chief of Staff.

Without looking up from his doodling: 'The sooner I get a scout patrol out on the far side of the Sun, the happier I'll be.'

'You accept Sir John's reconstruction?' asked the Minister.

'Not unreservedly,' said the Chief of Staff, looking up. 'I'd rather say it's a fair possibility, and one we ought to act on. Look, put it this way; sheer prudence demands we take this strange Fanshawe message seriously. Although it's a bit lurid, isn't it,' he said, picking up a sheet of paper and reading: ' "If this ship returns to Earth, then mankind is in deadly peril. God help you!" '

'Let's hope it isn't as bad as that,' said the Minister.

'The one thing I'm really worried about is our lack of radar range. It just isn't enough, not to deal with a full-scale attack from space. This is something I was talking to you about the other day, Sir John.' The Chief of Staff got up and walked to a large wall chart showing the planetary orbits. He moved the pointer around. 'What I'd like to do is to be able to cover distances as far out as Neptune at least—in all directions,' he said, decisively.

'Just remind me on one point,' said the Minister. 'How is it that our radar beams aren't strong enough to detect ships as far out as Neptune?'

'Two reasons. We have to detect ships by radar, and radar is a two-way affair. The radio waves travel outwards to the ship you want to find, the ship then reflects them, and you proceed to pick up these waves. When you're guiding a ship the signals only have to go one way—the waves only have to travel from Earth to the ship, which makes life a lot easier. Besides, you can put a much bigger transmitter on the ground and there are no limits on space or electrical power.'

'I don't quite understand why we couldn't use massive ground-based radar,' said the Minister thoughtfully.

'Well,' went on the Chief of Staff, 'because of the Sun. It gives out strong radio waves which swamp weak reflections from ships in its direction. Of course we can use ground-based stuff for the other directions, but we're forced to put ships right on the far side of the Sun—otherwise we'd be completely blind on that side.'

'Radar must always look away from the Sun, never into it,' said the Minister.

'Exactly. It's the same for radar as it is for ordinary light—the Sun is too bright,' the Chief of Staff said, looking at me.

'I see,' said the Minister. 'Except for one point. Ships over on the opposite side of the Sun may be able to cover directions we can't from Earth, but what good is that? Information can't be sent through to Earth because the Sun lies in the way.'

'It sounds very convincing, but there is an answer,' said Sir John smiling.

'There certainly is,' said the Chief of Staff, alert and precise. 'Our ships can send us information even past the Sun, because that part of the job is only a one-way affair! It's the reflected signals which are the weak ones.'

'Yes, yes. I see it now. The trouble with your patrol ships—the ones sent to the far side of the Sun—is that even from there they can't see far enough into space.'

'Yes, that's it. That's it exactly. The trouble is we

33

can't get much beyond Jupiter, and I'd really like to get at least as far as Neptune,' said the Chief of Staff emphatically as he sat down.

'May I interrupt for a moment?' said Sir John. 'Dr Warboys here has been developing a new transmitting valve, one that could greatly increase radar range.'

'Dr Warboys,' the Minister said, looking round at me.

'Yes, Minister,' I replied.

'You have a new device that might be of help to us in this problem of radar penetration?' said the Minister.

I was about to reply when the Chief of Staff said: 'Excuse me a moment; would you mind if one of my men sits in on this? If anything comes of the new transmitting valve, it'll probably be Colonel Rhodes who'll have the job of getting it operational.'

'Certainly. Please call Colonel Rhodes,' said the Minister to his secretary. 'Tell me, why are you so keen on Neptune as a yardstick in this business?' went on the Minister.

'Well, let us just suppose for a moment that a fleet of ships—hostile ships if you like—are really coming in towards the Earth. Then obviously the terrestrial battle fleet must be got into defensive positions around the Earth.'

'Obviously,' said the Minister.

'Well, you can't get upwards of five thousand ships out into space in five minutes.'

'How long d'you need in fact?' asked Sir John.

'In a crisis, three days. For preference, at least a week,' said the Chief of Staff.

'And that means detection as far as Neptune?' said Sir John.

'Quite right, Sir John. Assume a steady deceleration is planned to give a shut-down in velocity by the time the Sun is reached—or the Earth, for that matter. If you work it out for yourself, you'll find it comes to not much more than a week, a week from Neptune.'

'I'll take your word for it,' said the Minister, looking at me.

I was about to ask what happened if there were creatures who could withstand higher forces of deceleration, but thought better of it when I saw the expression on Sir John's face. At this moment the lift doors opened and into the room stepped Colonel Rhodes.

'Please take a seat, Colonel Rhodes,' said the Minister. 'Dr Warboys has come up with a new transmitting valve,' said the Chief of Staff, waving his hand in my direction. 'Colonel Rhodes, it's possible that you'll be involved in a space patrol in the near future. It will be of the utmost importance to have the best possible radar range. Dr Warboys here may possess a device that will enable you to improve the range we have at present,' finished the Chief of Staff.

'Dr Warboys,' said the Minister, turning to me. 'Does your new transmitting valve differ in principle or detail from existing devices?'

'It's a klystron tube modified in a somewhat unusual way. The increase of power output is surprisingly great, more than I'd hoped for.'

'What's the amount of the increase?' the Chief of Staff asked.

'I'd say a factor of thirty.'

'You mean your new transmitting valve is thirty times more powerful than existing ones?' said the Minister.

'Yes,' I replied.

'Then why hasn't this valve been put into use?' said the Minister.

'Lack of development,' I blurted out.

'That's ridiculous!'

'The new valve was being developed for the new radio the Space Council is building. Unfortunately the whole project is suffering a period of disinterest from the various governments involved, so there is very little money available,' Sir John explained my predicament.

'Well, this is most unfortunate, Dr Warboys,' the Minister said and added, turning to the Chief of Staff, 'Is this what you're looking for?'

'Absolutely. Just what we need. If it works, we'll be able to get quite close to the range we need.'

'Can this new valve be fitted into our existing radar systems?' asked Colonel Rhodes briskly.

'I don't see why not. But without precise details of the layout of your ships I couldn't say for certain.'

'Gentlemen. I think this is a matter for Dr Warboys and Colonel Rhodes to thrash out by themselves straight away,' said the Chief of Staff.

'I agree entirely,' said Sir John.

'Good, then this is the situation. We can give you fellows a few hours—no more—to find out if this new equipment can be fitted into an existing radar system. Now is there anything either of you wishes to ask?' said the Minister.

'No, I think everything's quite clear,' I said.

'As soon as I can see the valve, we'll know what the situation is,' Rhodes said getting to his feet. I followed suit.

'There's military transport available, Dr Warboys,' said the Chief of Staff.

'Thank you,' I said. It would save time if we were going to hurry back to Cambridge.

Everyone seemed to nod his approval and the signal for our departure.

'How serious is it?' Rhodes said as the lift descended.

'I just don't know, but you must have been involved in a few panics in the past.' I was noncommittal.

Rhodes was very direct. 'Ganges told me what you found before I came up to town. Do you have any idea of what might have happened to Fanshawe and his men?'

'Not really. It's anyone's guess at the moment,' I said, dodging the question.

The lift came to its silent stop. The doors opened and Rhodes marched off down one of the many corridors. About half-way down the passage he stopped, which gave me time to catch up. He was standing waiting for another lift. When I arrived at this point the lift doors opened, revealing a great big notice on the inside which said:

VEHICLES. MILITARY PERSONNEL ONLY.

37

Rhodes smiled at me as I read the notice. 'New people to the ministry were always using the lift, so the notice was stuck up.'

'Why not put it on the wall outside the lift?'

'Simple. We'd have all the political big wigs wanting free transport facilities. That's why we had the lift placed half-way down the corridor rather than at the ends with all the other lifts.'

'I suppose we all have our problems.'

Rhodes laughed. The lift stopped and we stepped out on to a roof top overlooking the Whitehall area. At a quick glance it seemed to be the only building in the park. A manually operated helicopter sat looking rather squat in comparison with the automatic computerized ones.

'Is it still safe to fly these manually?' I said, climbing in.

'Well, we do have trouble with the civil authorities over air corridors, but they are instructed to keep out of our manual flying zone. The police are the worst; they seem to use all the available flying space whether it is necessary or not,' Rhodes said, firing up the machine.

I noticed with amusement that he put on the protective flying helmet with radio transmitting equipment in it.

'Just in case the computers are re-routing helicopters. I can call them up and tell them there's a war on,' Rhodes shouted above the noise.

A couple of police and ambulance helicopters narrowly missed us as we banked sharply and set off north towards Cambridge.

Rhodes was saying something but I couldn't hear him. In desperation he handed me another helmet, and I put it on.

At first there was complete silence. Rhodes looked at me. I shook my head negatively. He fiddled with some knobs and then I was on the air.

The tall chimney of the University Library was now visible.

'My labs are to the west of that library spire up ahead,' I said.

'You mean on the vast science complex,' Rhodes said a little sadly.

'I'm afraid so; gone are the days of laboratories in dark smelly corners.'

'Hold on,' Rhodes said, with a mischievous smile on his face. The helicopter banked sharply and then turned upside down. In this mad attitude we progressed to the landing area within the science complex. Some students below pointed upwards. My head was full of blood, and my stomach began to feel rather unsettled. Rhodes somehow managed to get us the right way up before landing.

'Sorry about that,' Rhodes said as we got out of the helicopter. My legs felt like jelly. 'I used to be in the Aerobatics team when I first learned to fly,' came the sympathetic voice as Rhodes caught my arm. 'Which way?' he said.

I pointed in the direction of the lab, and set off with Rhodes in tow.

The door was locked. No students here today, I thought crossly to myself and pressed the key reader with my forefinger.

'Is that one of the new locks?' Rhodes asked, as the catch unmagnetized itself. I pushed the door open and we went in.

'Yes,' I said. 'Very simple and foolproof. There's a small computer next to the main one on the complex here, which operates all or virtually all the locks.'

'What activates it?'

'Fingerprints, only those authorized have check prints in the computer which opens the door. Other people pressing the button only ring the bell,' I said proudly.

'What happens if someone else makes you press the button?'

'We have an emergency procedure which alerts the guard and also photographs the intruders, together with other subtle devices for identification,' I said, going over to my wall safe. Inside was the developing part of the camera. I took the exposed film, tore off the developing papers and there was a picture of Rhodes and myself.

'It's very good. Hope they hurry up and get these installed at the military base, then I'll know who's raiding my drink cupboard.'

While Rhodes looked round the lab, I took the new valve and the transparent tube containing a metallic wave guide, and started fitting them together.

'Fascinating place. Is this it?' Rhodes said, putting his finger on the tube.

'Yes. The object of this part of the equipment is to get the power matched into the wave guide.'

'Is the wave guide standard? I'm thinking about linking up with our aerial feed,' Rhodes asked.

'There'll have to be a tunable coupling unit, but I can provide that,' I said.

'Good. There appear to be no insuperable difficulties in getting it into one of our space destroyers. How long would it take to fit?' said Rhodes, doing some hand measurements.

The telephone started buzzing.

'I'll get it,' said Rhodes. He flicked the switch and the Chief of Staff came up on the screen.

'Colonel Rhodes. We've decided to send your group out immediately with the new radar equipment.'

'Yes, sir.'

'Warboys, how long will it take you to fit?'

'Several days, I should think,' I replied.

'Fine, it is now 12.52. You will take off at 15.00 hours. Will this give you time?' said the Chief of Staff.

'Yes, I think so,' I said.

'Good. Colonel, you'll be responsible for anything Dr Warboys needs.'

'Yes, sir,' said Rhodes, then the phone went dead.

'Amazing. What would happen if the valve is no good?' I said.

'The Military don't worry about that. It's just got to work,' Rhodes said. He laughed at the look of dismay and horror spreading on my face. I'd just realized they were going to fire me into space.

41

4

Rhodes left the lab shortly after the conversation with his Chief of Staff, and went to Mildenhall to arrange for his own space craft to be brought by rail from Stansted. This way the rest of his group would take off from Stansted while we could take off from Mildenhall, allowing me more time to organize myself.

I put all the equipment that I'd need into a tool box and carefully packed up the valve and wave guides. I wrote a message on the blackboard for my students telling them I'd be away for a few days, picked up my tool box and guides and returned to College. Once there I hurriedly changed into a pair of working overalls. As I finished zipping myself in there was a buzz from the door bell.

A young soldier stood to attention on the doorstep. 'Are you ready, sir?' he said, as I opened the door to let him in.

'Yes,' I said and after a glance round, we left. He had kept the helicopter running. I put the tool box behind my seat and got in.

'Would you mind fastening your safety harness, sir?' said the driver as we took off.

'Why?' I said with curiosity.

'There's a strong wind coming up from the south-west, and my orders are to get you to Mildenhall without incident,' said the young man.

At around two hundred feet I began to realize what he meant. The manual helicopters had no stabilizing gyros on them and the strong wind was throwing us around like a small ship in a typhoon.

On arrival I felt very seasick. The driver put the helicopter neatly down almost on top of Colonel Ganges' well-polished boots. Ganges took one look at me and then roared with laughter.

'Man, you look terrible,' Ganges said, still laughing.

'Thank you for those few words of encouragement,' I said, with as much coldness as I could muster. Ganges just guffawed.

The destroyer stood on the concrete not far from the DSP 15 exploratory space craft. The crews of those early ships must have had immense courage to fly into the unknown with a ship as frail as the DSP 15, in comparison with Rhodes' bull-nosed ship. The driver stood a little way off with my tool box and guides in his hand.

'How long do you think it will be before you have this valve gadget working?' Ganges said, as we moved off towards the ship.

'I'm not sure. I suppose the slower we go the better,' I said, pondering on Ganges' expression.

'Don't think you'll be travelling much slower than usual,' said Ganges.

'Why?' I said, wondering what travelling in a space ship would be like.

44

'The orders are to proceed as quickly as possible to your observing point along with the rest of the group from Stansted.'

'Well, I suppose I'll be able to manage,' I said, beginning to feel a few misgivings at volunteering for such an operation. Surely there were good army electronic engineers who could do this job. Did it really need a physicist?

We reached the destroyer. Ganges stretched out his hand. 'Good luck.'

'Thanks, you shouldn't be so pessimistic about things.'

He grunted.

The young soldier who'd brought me from Cambridge handed over my equipment. I stepped on to the outside lift platform, pressed the button and was shot skywards, which didn't help the sick feeling in my stomach.

'Hello, Warboys,' said Rhodes, greeting me at the small hatch.

'Here,' I said, handing him my gear. 'I think you'd better call me Dick.'

'All right, mine's Colonel.'

'You're what!' I said, banging my head against the low ceiling in the air lock.

'My father was always very military minded. He was very disillusioned at having two daughters, so when I came along he must have been very excited and confused, as my birth certificate is registered as "Colonel Rhodes",' Rhodes said with a chuckle.

'What an introduction. Colonel Colonel Rhodes,' I said with great amusement.

45

Colonel led the way down a short passage that went from the outside door to the middle of the ship. Here there was a lift that served the ship from top to bottom. Colonel closed the gate and we moved leisurely upwards for a short distance.

'We'll drop your equipment off here,' he said, opening up the gate and moving into a largish room. This was obviously the communications part of the ship. There was a computer, and masses of electronic devices. 'I'll leave your stuff here,' Colonel said, pointing to a cupboard labelled 'Radar'.

He came back to the lift, and we continued upwards.

'What happens if the lift goes wrong?' I asked.

'Oh, each floor has safety hatches so we can get from one to another without using the lift.'

The upward motion stopped and we walked into the main cabin. It was very simply laid out; one half of the circle had contoured bunks with a small table of instruments and monitor screen. The other half of the circle was covered by the main control panel. A movable chair was fixed near the centre of the panel, which I assumed was the Captain's.

'This way, Dick,' said Colonel, taking me by the arm. I went with him, over to a large cabinet. 'Here we have all the emergency equipment.' Inside were hanging space suits and helmets. Behind these were some space bikes and jet packs for propelling oneself around.

'This is your suit and propulsion pack,' said Colonel, showing me a single dull grey suit and black pack. The others, both suits and packs, were white.

46

'Am I likely to need it?' I asked, fingering the rubbery material of the suit.

'No, but it's a precautionary measure we take; remember you're in military hands now,' he said with a smile.

'What happens if there's a fire?' I said jokingly.

'You'll know about it. Bells ring and you grab your suit and get yourself plugged into the oxygen supply as fast as you can.'

I looked at a junction box in the control panel that was labelled 'Oxygen'.

'Otherwise you'll get gassed. The first whiff of smoke and the nearest hydrant starts operating.'

'Marvellous. So you don't do any live cooking?' I said, looking around while the crew went about their jobs taking no notice of my naïve questions. 'What are those?' I said, pointing at some metal discs high up in the ceiling.

'For getting at the armoury. Torpedoes mainly, but there are some side arms and grenades,' Colonel said, as he checked some instruments on the control panel.

'Torpedo tubes. Are we carrying them?' I asked.

'Certainly,' came the reply.

'Five minutes to zero,' said one of the crew. Rhodes nodded in the man's direction, and then went over to the bunks.

'This is very simple,' Colonel said, starting to fasten me down on one of them with cross straps. The other crewmen came over and lay down on their bunks. I noticed that they only used one stomach strap instead of the three I was held down by.

'This button here alters the height of the head rest. This one turns you around, and this one raises or lowers your feet,' Colonel said, pushing the various buttons he was talking about. The bunk rode up and down like a horse on the run.

Colonel left me in approximately the same position as I'd started in, facing towards the control panel. He walked across to his chair and settled himself in. The chair in fact turned out to be a bunk, for the back rest folded flat, followed by the foot rest coming up level. 'You see, Dick, it's all very civilized,' he said, swinging himself round as a child would.

I pressed the head rest button curiously. Slowly my head came up so I could get a better look at the cabin.

'Two minutes to zero,' crackled a voice, which resounded round the metal walls. Suddenly I felt as though I couldn't breathe.

'It's all right, Dr Warboys. We've just changed over to our own oxygen supply,' said a voice near me. I nodded and wondered what I must have looked like to promote this piece of information.

'What do you do?' I said feebly.

'I'm the communications officer,' said the young man lying on the bunk next to me.

'Zero,' crackled the voice out of the intercom.

I felt as though I was rising in an ultra fast lift. Then suddenly as if someone was slowly flattening me with a giant press.

I must have blacked out, for the next thing I remember was everyone busily going about his duties.

48

'Whew, I'm glad that's over,' I said, unbelting myself.

'It's always like that the first trip. Be careful, you'll find walking a little strange,' Colonel said.

I swung my legs off the bunk and stood up. My legs just folded under me and I grabbed at the bunk.

'You all right?' Colonel said, beginning to get up from his chair.

I nodded and tried again. This time everything worked, although I reeled towards the control panel like a drunk.

'It may be a bit of a consolation to know that take-off never gets much better however long you're in the game. Here, take a look at the Earth,' said Colonel putting a picture up on one of the monitors. From somewhere behind me I felt a chair pushed under my unsteady seat.

'Superb. The delicacy of colours,' I said after a long studied look. I felt as though I might never feel real ground under my feet again.

'Yes. Photographs never seem quite the same. Cloud, desert, pole-caps and oceans. You'll find it looks even better on the way home,' Colonel said with a twinkle in his eyes.

'I'll bet,' I said fervently. Colonel proceeded to flick some switches.

'Redscout calling Edelweiss. Redscout calling Edelweiss. Over,' said Colonel.

A moment later a Germanic voice came crackling back.

'Edelweiss receiving you, over.'

'Edelweiss. Your instructions are as follows. Take the group at maximum speed to heliocentric longitude 217°, centi-astronomical units 92. I'll follow a day behind. Over,' said Colonel.

'Edelweiss calling. Group to Helio 217. Cow 92. What's wrong, Redscout? Got a weak stomach? Over,' came the crackling reply.

'Stomach O.K. Job to do. Get on course. Roger,' said Colonel, flicking the switches back into position. 'I'll be accelerating at normal gravity, 1 g. instead of the usual operational 1.5 g. to give you the best conditions for working. But I'll be hooking the old bus inside Venus, so we're going to fry, in spite of the air conditioners. They aren't very good in these fast destroyers, I'm afraid. Everything has been cut down for the sake of speed.'

'Fine. Can I go and have a look at the works downstairs?' I asked, wondering what Colonel meant by frying.

'Certainly, you go ahead, and if you want me there's an intercom on the wall by the door. Otherwise the ship's yours at the moment.'

I went over to the lift. It shot down and upset my stomach yet again. I wondered whether it was really absolutely necessary to send me in the lift to the bottom of the shaft while under acceleration. The door opened and I was in the communications room. Life felt reasonably good now, or at least till I got the back off the radar control unit. Typical, I thought; although there was an instruction card, someone had done repairs ignoring the colour coding used to distinguish parts.

A couple of hours later, or at least that's what it felt like, as my watch had suffered in take off, I was beginning to see where I was going and it didn't take me long to get the valve wired up. The bigger problem was going to be the tunable coupling unit for the aerial feed.

The lift doors opened and Colonel Rhodes came in. 'How's it going?' he asked.

'Well, if your electronics engineers stuck to the proper colour coding, life would be that much simpler,' I said.

'Sorry about that. I see you're sorting things out though. How are you finding it down here?'

'Hot, but I've been so busy I've not had much time to complain,' I said, suddenly realizing that I was sweating like a rainy day and there were wet patches on the floor. I stood up easing my back into a more comfortable position. 'What's the time?'

'Earth time. Around 03.00 hours.'

'Grief! How long have I been down here?'

'About eight hours or so. How much longer do you think you'll be?'

'An hour or two. Strange that I don't feel very tired.'

'You shouldn't feel tired, you had a nice long nap at lift off,' said Colonel with a smile.

'Now I've stopped work, I see what you mean about the heat. Do you feel it as much as I do?'

'I'm more used to putting up with it than you.

Another few hours and we'll be over the worst. Better take a look at Venus. She's not very far away—to starboard.' Colonel turned on the monitor. 'There it is. The devil planet. Cold as Nordic hell on the outside, hot as Mediterranean hell down at its surface.'

'So those are the famous dry-ice clouds?' I said.

'Yes,' said Colonel. 'When you get under them the light seems to come at you from all sides. Nothing seems right. Just great expanses of dusty desert, everything's unreal. Six months down there and you're as nutty as a March Hare.'

I gave an involuntary shiver and got back to work.

'Message from Edelweiss, sir. Squadron nearing rendezvous,' came a voice from the intercom.

'Good, better contact Edelweiss. Tell him we're nearing rendezvous point,' said Colonel.

'I'll be ready soon,' I said, having found a place to cut in the tunable coupling unit.

'Good. Do you feel hungry?' asked Colonel as he got into the lift. I nodded and the doors closed.

I suppose it took me about an hour or so to fix the coupling unit. When all the bits and pieces had been tidied up, I wrote on the colour chart: 'WORK THIS ONE OUT'.

'Finished?' Colonel inquired, as I emerged from the lift.

'I hope so. Where's this food you were talking about?'

'Here,' he said, pointing to a couple of delicious looking blue and yellow tablets.

'What are they?'

'Steak and chips. Double rations?'

'How about liquid?' I said, swallowing the pills. A crewman handed me a container with a tube coming out from the top. I sucked and to my delight it really was hot sweet coffee.

'Do you think you'll be able to give me distance and speed?' Colonel asked.

'Certainly. But one thing bothers me. Not the equipment, but the way you military people do your sums. You ask me for radar detection out to Neptune. It seems strange to me how you can be sure that's really far enough. Any craft coming into our Solar System must begin deceleration at a distance far out beyond Neptune,' I said.

'Fair question. In fact almost a hundred times farther out. By the time a ship reaches Neptune we expect it to have checked speed to about three per cent of light,' said Colonel, looking at the monitor.

'So the additional deceleration as the ship comes in to Earth cuts the speed right down to nothing at all, I suppose?' I mused.

'That's right.'

'Then you must be working on the basis of a steady deceleration of about 1 g. If we were really up against something unusual, how can you be sure that the space crafts we might be dealing with can't manage a deceleration of 10 g.?'

'What sort of creature could stand up to 10 g. for weeks on end? They'd have to be very small creatures!' Colonel said rather cynically.

'You mean a rat might be able to stand up to a big deceleration, but a rat couldn't design a space ship.'

'That's right.'

I found the radar aerial unit and turned everything on, so as to give it final adjustment.

'I'll admit it looks like a good argument. I only hope it turns out as good as it looks,' I said thoughtfully, helping myself to another sip of coffee, and watching the needles flickering and creeping up from zero.

'Edelweiss on the blower, sir. Says everyone is in position. He'd like a word with you,' said the communications officer.

'Fine,' said Colonel, opening up the channel and putting it on the intercom by flicking a switch in front of him.

'Redscout calling Edelweiss. Redscout calling Edelweiss, over.'

'Hey, Redscout. Who in hell's name have they got in Huntsman? Over.'

'I don't know. Over.'

'Better find out. Sounds crazy to me. Over and out.'

'Get me Huntsman,' said Colonel.

'Yes, sir. Redscout calling Huntsman. Redscout calling Huntsman. Over.'

Not a sound. Colonel looked round at everyone.

'Redscout calling Huntsman. Over,' went on the communications officer.

'Huntsman here. Tally ho! Excruciatin' speed. Over.'

'Carry on, Huntsman. Over and out.' Colonel flicked the switch and turned with an enormous smile on his

54

face. 'How on earth did old Ganges get himself into this show?'

'I should imagine by his quite infallible recipe of cutting through red tape,' I said, laughing.

'Big flare on the Sun, sir,' said a voice from beside me.

'Everyone into the protection compartment, don't waste time,' Rhodes yelled, dragging me with him.

Once the heavy door closed we looked like pilchards in a can.

'We're surrounded by thicker material here to give us protection from X-Rays. They're produced in the skin of the rocket, by the storm of high energy particles from the flare,' said Colonel.

Suddenly there was a terrifying banging and clattering.

'Lucky the spectrum cuts off pretty sharply. Otherwise this protection wouldn't be much use. Ever had a ship completely cooked by a really bad storm?' I asked.

'Charlie Odgers and his crew were badly burned in a big storm three years ago,' one of the crew piped up.

The dials on the wall were beginning to dance.

'Near sunspot maximum, things can be pretty dicey. Here it comes,' said Colonel, looking at the dials where the needles were beginning to bang up against the maximum stop. 'We'll just have to sweat it out for a few hours until the monitors go off.'

I must have gone off to sleep, as the next thing I knew was Colonel shaking me. The crew had left the compartment. I got up and moved into the main cabin.

55

Everything there was still and normal, but we were steaming wet as if fully clothed in a Turkish bath.

'Have you very much more to do?' asked Colonel.

'No, just the final touches. Is the aerial turning?'

'Is the aerial turning?' Colonel repeated.

'Aerial turning,' called a crewman.

I made my final adjustments.

'No signals?' asked Colonel.

'No, only from the rest of the group,' said the crewman.

'Well, she seems to have passed the first test. The power will come up gradually.' I began to tidy up. Everyone gathered round the display tube.

'She's only at a quarter power,' I said, going over to where Colonel and the others were standing.

'How far out are we going, would you say?'

'A bit beyond Saturn.'

'About twice our normal range. There doesn't seem to be much out there,' said Colonel.

'I'm not so sure, sir. Look over here,' said one of the crewmen. 'I thought I saw a spot, but it could be just noise.'

We followed his finger.

'I don't see anything, but your eyes are probably better than mine for this sort of thing,' said Colonel.

The power gauge was now showing half power.

'I think there is something,' said the communications officer excitedly.

'Yes, my God. I can see it now,' said Colonel.

'It's breaking up—into scores of blips, sir.'

'The transmitter is now at full power,' I said.

'How many dots?' Colonel's voice barked.

'Difficult to say, sir, but a lot. Could be a hundred, could be thousands. Can't say, sir.'

'It's a fleet of ships,' I said amazed.

'And not disposed to be friendly either, Dick.'

'How do you figure that?' I said, studying the display tube.

Colonel put his finger on the tube. 'Look where they're coming in. Bang in the plane of the planets, bang in a direction opposite to Earth.'

'You mean they're coming into Earth right out of the direction of the Sun?'

'Yes, just like our great-grandfathers used to do in the old air battles. Can you give me coordinates?' Colonel said, turning to a crewman.

'I've been checking. They're spreading out between heliocentric longitudes 33.5 to 44,' came the reply.

Colonel wrote down Helio 33.5 to 44 on a piece of paper.

'2793 centi-astronomical units, sir.'

Colonel wrote this down too. 'Dick, can you give me their speed? That's the critical thing.'

'A bit above 12,000 miles per second,' I said, working madly at the calculation.

'Impossible!'

'No,' I said, rechecking the figures.

'What does it mean, sir?'

'It means the creatures in those ships are taking a steady deceleration not of 1 g. but of 3 g. And they've

57

been taking it for several weeks on end,' I said, looking once more at my calculations.

'Can't understand it,' Colonel muttered. 'Only little creatures could take 3 g. continuously. There's something wrong, somewhere.'

'Nothing's wrong,' I said. 'We now know that rats can build space craft.'

Colonel looked at me, and then at the radar screen. 'Get me Earth,' he said quietly.

5

It took nearly half an hour to make contact with Earth, and we were all thoroughly tense and irritated by the time we heard a crackling voice that sounded very far away:

'Hello, Redscout. World Space Control here, over.'

'Hello, Space Control, where the devil have you been? Over.'

'Sorry, Redscout. Equipment malfunctional, over.'

'Damned fools, always having servicing problems,' Colonel said to us in the ship. 'We have contacted enemy fleet coming in at 2793 centi-astronomical units, over.'

'How many?'

'Couldn't say, except that it's a large number.'

'Are you absolutely sure of this?'

'We've recalculated and there is definitely an alien force coming in towards Earth. And they are decelerating at 3 g.'

'Impossible!'

'We've been watching them for over an hour now. Dr Warboys and I agree that they are coming in at 3 g.'

There was a moment's silence. Lots of static. Then a

voice said: 'Hello, Redscout. This is Lt-General Sir Robert Milner.'

'Chief of Staff,' Colonel said to me.

'Colonel Rhodes, are you certain of this? Over.'

'Sir, we have checked and rechecked and there is no doubt about it, over.'

'Right. The various destroyer groups up now will have to make a stand while we get the main world fleet off the ground.'

'O.K., sir. Message understood. What about Warboys?'

'Can't be helped, do your best. Over and out,' said the Chief of Staff.

'I'm sorry, Dick,' said Colonel. He looked strained.

'Don't worry. Your Chief of Staff made up my mind for me. Are we fully operational now?'

'Well. It will take them about three days to get the whole fleet up. Our job will be to observe, pass back information.'

'What usually happens to the forward fleet?'

'We've never had to find out, but in this case we keep out of the way for as long as possible.'

I felt a little sick. Military men are perhaps reasonably conditioned to dying, but to a civilian the idea of one's corpse floating round in space doesn't really appeal.

Colonel had a large map of our solar system illuminated on the wall.

'One thing that strikes me is these enemy ships will

be far more vulnerable than yours,' I said, looking at the map.

'Hm. You're probably right.'

'How will we fight?' I asked, trying to break into the train of thought that would be running through Colonel and the crew's minds.

'There's only one thing we can really do—dispose our forces in a tight ball, between Venus and Mars, with Earth more or less in the centre,' Colonel said, indicating on the map with his finger. 'The idea is to keep the enemy on the far side, so he has to cover more distance than we do.'

'Where does this leave us?' I asked.

'Well, the enemy is nearly inside the orbit of Jupiter. We are on the far side of the Sun—about here,' Colonel pointed. 'By now I should think they'll have withdrawn half the other forward groups, back towards Earth.'

'Which means that we're going to be taking the brunt of everything?' I said, realizing more fully what was happening.

'Yes,' said Colonel philosophically.

'These torpedoes, are they any good?'

'I shouldn't think so. If these fellows can decelerate at 3 g. then they can probably outshoot us, but I think we might give them a bit of a surprise,' Colonel said with a smile. 'Where are they?'

'They're coming round the Sun, sir,' said a crewman from the radar screen.

'Well, they're not missing out on this trick. They're coming up to see if anybody's here.'

I looked at the screen.

'That's it,' said Colonel snapping his fingers. 'They're going to pick off our radar outposts—that's us. I'd say we've got about five hours before they're on to us.'

'What's to be done, sir?' said a crewman.

'There's one chance. Dick, do you think you could do a bit of wizardry with electric circuits in our torpedoes?'

'In what way?' I asked.

'To make a whole salvo hunt together, instead of each torpedo hunting singly, one at a time.'

'How do you mean?'

'I want to attack a single target with a full broadside and I want it done like this. If the first torpedo misses, as it probably will—I want it to feed information to the second one, so it won't make the same mistake. If the second one misses then it must send all its information to the third—and so on. It'll enormously increase the chance of a hit first shot.'

'Why aren't your torpedoes automatically fixed up like this?' I asked.

'Normally it'd be too wasteful. It'll mean we fire off half our stuff all in one go.'

'Why do you want to do this, sir?' said a crewman.

'I want to make the enemy think our shooting is a lot better than it really is. I want a hit first shot—whatever the cost in ammunition.'

'You're hoping that after that they might leave us alone?'

'Right. Can you do it, Dick?'

'I can try,' I said.

The crew members found a ladder and opened up one of the hatches in the ceiling. One of them was sent for my tool box. All equipped, I climbed up the ladder and through the hatch. I looked for the service card; what I needed was an inter-connection between the torpedo and the radar equipment. At length I found what I wanted. There was a link between the two. Whoever designed the torpedo equipment had had this in mind, as the links were there but not connected up. The torpedoes were so designed that, once the torpedo had been fired, it was fed information about the target by radio waves from the ship, which was, in turn, picking up information on its radar equipment. Now I could also arrange an over-riding signal from the torpedoes in sequence.

The problem had turned out to be easier than I had hoped.

I was two hours cooped up in that small space, tense and hot, but with a hope at least. At last I climbed down the ladder. Below all the crew were wearing their silver space suits. Colonel indicated my suit, which was lying on a bunk, and one of the crew came over to help me on with it and set up my respirator.

'How did it go?' Colonel's voice came through the headpiece.

'Not quite perfect, but I think there should be some fireworks.'

'Good enough,' said Colonel.

I moved over towards the radar screen. Colonel got

up and came over to join me. There were eight blobs of light approaching us at high speed.

'Shall I try the radio, sir?'

'No.'

'Torpedo coming in to port,' came the call from the communications officer.

The monitors flashed, and then the whole ship did a bit of an Irish jig.

I picked myself up off the floor. Colonel was still standing on his feet. I couldn't understand that.

'A miss, but not by much,' he said, going over to the flight control panel.

'I'm taking her in.'

Suddenly the whole of my headpiece was full of static and weird babblings. I shook my head, but the sound didn't go. The ship lunged again, and then it felt as though we'd done a complete somersault.

'They're getting too near. I daren't risk closing any further. All ready for firing?'

'Yes, sir.'

'Setting—Green 19.113—Red 472.6—Yellow 9,3001. Rates—0.4467—0.0133—0.2426,' said one of the crew watching the dials.

'Fire,' Colonel shouted. I shook my head as the noise of Colonel's voice plus the babbling became even more oppressive. The destroyer checked for a fraction of a second as the torpedoes left the ship.

Suddenly I was flung back on the floor. Not by an explosion, but by Colonel changing course. He was trying to outmanoeuvre the enemy destroyers. Then the severe pressure of acceleration at around 5 g. stopped.

'Are you all right, Dick?' said Colonel.

'The way I feel, it wasn't worth while,' I said, picking up my bruised body off the floor.

'Come and take a look.'

I went over to the radar screen and had a look. There were only seven ships.

'Only seven ships,' Colonel said, slapping me on the back.

'Good.'

I still felt violently sick. Someone shouted. They were coming in again. Colonel fired the second salvo, and again that agonizing acceleration.

'Sir, there's another fleet coming in,' said Sparks.

I looked up from my undignified position on the floor.

'Another fleet!' Colonel said.

'Yes, sir. Coming in at heliocentric longitude 45°.'

The ship throttled back, which allowed me to move around.

'That's damned queer,' Colonel said. 'One fleet coming in from port and the other from starboard, and we're smack in the middle.'

'What's so odd about that?' I said feebly.

'Well, this second fleet must have been out of radar contact with the first, the Sun was between them. We're going to be crushed between the two.'

Everyone looked inquiringly at Colonel.

'Signal the information back to Earth,' he said to the communications officer.

'So we're finished,' I said, realizing that as every minute went by the possible chance of our survival diminished.

'I'm sorry, Dick. It was the best I could do,' Colonel said, turning to his Sparks. 'How many ships are answering the transponder?'

'About 217, sir,' came the reply.

'They might as well save lives,' said the Colonel rather gloomily.

The ship started spinning as a torpedo exploded near by. Then another explosion. At the third explosion everyone was thrown from one end of the cabin to the other. The instrument panel shorted out, and the lights went.

'We've been hit, sir.'

Colonel didn't have time to say anything as the ship was hit again. Everything disintegrated, the crew went flying through space at different angles.

It is a strange sensation to spin slowly through space at a constant speed, which one doesn't feel. Eventually I gave up the struggle to stabilize, and started to concentrate on myself. There didn't seem to be any serious injuries. My main worry was having a damaged suit, but I wouldn't be alive if the suit was ripped, so I gingerly moved my limbs to see if any bones were broken and decided that I was only bruised.

The battle, from what I could see from my strange topsy turvy flight through space, was still going on. But strangely it looked as if the second fleet was attacking the first. Was that possible? It must be my eyesight or some form of brain damage. An absurd fear was mounting in me that, in floating away from the battle area, any chance of my being picked up was lost.

Suddenly a new problem arose. An alien ship coming straight at me. Well, that's it, I thought. But just as suddenly as it appeared it vanished. A curious and sad thought struck me. I would have liked to have seen the strange creatures inside before I passed on my way into the depths of our solar system.

As I spun round for about the millionth time, I noticed the dark shape of a ship lying not far off. My heart missed a beat. There was a flash of light and something went zipping by. I waited for an explosion, but nothing happened. I realized that the thing which had gone flying by was not a missile intended to destroy me, but a life line. The trouble was they'd missed, so the line was just out of reach. Another flash of light, and this time I found the line between my legs. The lack of gravity and loss of normal coordination made the effort of grabbing it monumental, but I slowly found a loop on my belt which opened and was able to attach the line through it. About five minutes later I noticed I'd changed direction. The life line was pulling me towards the ship. In my excitement at this discovery, I didn't question whether it was one of our fleet or an alien craft.

The line pulled me nearer. Was it one of ours? It looked thinner; I wasn't sure. Then I knew; this wasn't one of ours. The hatch that would normally be around the middle of the ship, was missing. This ship had the opening very near the exhaust end, and as I drew closer, I saw that the torpedo tubes were not in the nose section, but attached to the side. Inside my space suit I broke out in a cold sweat.

The hatch was a large double-door affair. The line pulled me in, through the outer doors, and right up to a point in the wall. The outer doors closed. An incandescent light glowed and I saw that the line had towed me into a large airlock. I began to float slowly to the floor. As I undid my life line, gravity seemed to increase gradually and my equilibrium began to come back. A few moments later a panel behind me slid quietly open and my taut nerves gave a twinge of fear. I walked unsteadily into another small cubicle.

Suddenly the floor seemed to come up at me, and I stumbled around trying to regain my balance. I laughed nervously as I realized this was a high speed lift. It stopped. Another moment's delay, then the panel slid back and I was looking into a brilliantly lit cabin at the alien crew. They moved forward. Some were wearing silver-coloured space suits, one was a brilliant emerald green colour and one was golden. At least they were about normal human height, but because of their dark visors, I couldn't see their faces. My surprise at seeing human shapes rather than 'rats' steadied me, but I was still nervous enough to jump when the thing in gold came over to me, took hold of my arm and led me from the lift. It was not a vicious authoritative grip, but more like a friendly gesture to a blind person. Once

68

out of the lift the door slid shut and I felt the fastener on my helmet being released. The chap in gold gave me a sort of O.K. sign and I took the helmet off. I held my breath as the helmet came off, but I had to breathe and to my relief the atmosphere seemed normal instead of the toxic mixture it might have been.

The whole crew began to take helmets off. They had human faces! I began to wonder whether they were in fact part of the Earth's space fleet.

'Selgain,' said the man in gold.

'Hello,' I said, nervously bracing myself. They all looked curiously at me. The gentleman in gold went over to a panel and pressed a button. A desk appeared. I was ushered over and invited to sit on a stool which appeared to be attached to the desk. They all crowded round me and I began to wonder what they wanted me to do. The fellow in gold then started to point to his mouth and moved his lips as though he was speaking.

'Do you want me to talk?' I said.

They all looked delighted.

'I think I begin to understand,' I said, warming to the job. 'You want me to talk, to see if you can find out what language I'm talking in. Well, I don't quite know how you're going to do this, but I hope you can. My name is Richard or Dick Warboys. I am a bachelor. I live in St John's College, Cambridge, England, and work at the University there.' I stopped. As I'd been talking a print-out machine had been working. At a guess I would think a computer was putting my speech patterns into numerical form. I talked on more carefully

69

and methodically. The chap in gold started studying the information. I looked round at the other crew members. The fellow in the green suit looked extraordinarily young. Suddenly I realized that it wasn't a man, it was a woman.

The fellow in gold took hold of a typing machine and started banging away on the keys. When he'd finished the print-out shot out its reply. He read it and then did some more typing.

'Selgain,' said the man, smiling. 'Greetings,' came his voice a fraction of a second later from the intercom.

'Greetings,' I said, which was followed by 'Selgain'.

The man in gold smiled and talked into the machine, which said: 'My name is Betelgeuse. This is Alcyone,' he brought the girl forward, she smiled. 'And this is Rigel.' Rigel nodded. 'And these are the three M's.' The three strapping young men nodded and said 'Selgain' as one man.

I nodded a greeting to them.

'You were very lucky,' said Betelgeuse, pointing to the belt on my space suit. 'It sent out a distress signal.'

I thanked my lucky stars. It must have been actuated automatically as I was ejected from the ship. 'Could you pick up the rest of my crew?' I asked.

'We can try. Can you show me where you were hit?' Betelgeuse asked.

He handed me a pointer, and a picture of the area with the dead and exploded ships marked appeared on an illuminated panel. From what I could remember we had been roughly at the point of a V. Our ships at the bottom, one fleet to the left, and someone coming in from the right. I looked hard and eventually could make out the original V. There at the bottom was marked an explosion.

'Here, I think,' I said, pointing.

Alcyone and Rigel went over to the typing machine, and punched something out. The ship started to move.

'We will make a circle of the area. Have you any idea of your speed at the time you were hit?'

'No,' I said. We might have been doing any speed at the time.

'Then we'll work on the speed you yourself were travelling at.'

We travelled a full circle without any success.

Betelgeuse looked at me. 'We will go into the exact area, but I'm afraid that, if there isn't anyone there, we must return you to Earth.'

'You will return me to Earth?' I asked.

'The Earth people are in great danger.'

'I can see.'

'Greater than I think you realize.'

'What do you mean?'

'When the time is right, you will know,' Betelgeuse said.

I wondered whether this was just a trick to find out about landing instructions on Earth. The intercom started to crackle with static. I thought I heard something. There it was, the old 'mayday' distress signal.

'What does it mean?' asked Alcyone.

'The signal?'

'Yes.'

'It means "Help me".'

'Very apt,' smiled Betelgeuse.

The signal kept getting stronger and stronger until we were almost on top of it. I watched a picture of the space outside. The viewer scanned until it fixed on a dark patch. The dark patch became a wreck. Then I saw it. A small image moved among the wrecked parts. Whoever it was had a space pack on his back, as I could see small spurts of flame occasionally. It became apparent as we watched, that whoever it was out there was making his way away from us.

'He's afraid of us,' Betelgeuse observed.

'Not surprising,' I said.

'You want me to bring him here?'

'Certainly. As long as you don't hurt him.'

I watched as they linked the man up on what I assumed was their target scope. A small rocket suddenly shot across the picture. Betelgeuse waited, looking a little tense.

'What's happened?' I said, trying to see what was going on outside.

'He's avoided the line.'

Betelgeuse lined up the target on the scope and then fired another small rocket. It seemed to go up to the target and then stop.

'You're watching a very simple little device,' Betelgeuse said with a smile. 'Since he doesn't want to be rescued, we'll bring him in with a little pressure.'

'What exactly is it?'

'A line that's used to clear wreckage in space. The rocket head is programmed to do whatever you want. You see it has arrived at its target, and it waits for further instructions. Now I turn on a strong magnetic field.'

'What a marvellous toy,' I said.

'Certainly, but it does the job.'

Betelgeuse pressed a button and the fellow outside must have got a shock, as he started moving backwards, but it wasn't long before the man was in the air-lock and coming up in the lift.

The door opened, and I moved forward in front of Betelgeuse and his crew. My thoughts were right. I moved in quickly. The man was holding a grenade. Before I could tackle him the man put the grenade back on his belt. He came out of the lift and started removing his helmet.

'Couldn't kill you, Dick,' said Colonel Rhodes. 'Have they grilled you yet?'

'No, they haven't. I hadn't even thought of that; they were going to return me to Earth if they hadn't found anyone else,' I said.

'Fiddlesticks, it's just a trick to find out what our landing procedure is.'

'Well, Betelgeuse, what have you to say to my friend's accusation?' I said.

'We could land without much trouble, but it would mean panic and distress. You call Earth and find out what they have to say.'

'What! Tell them to let you in. Oh, no!' Colonel said briskly.

Betelgeuse signalled something, and the ship started moving.

'What are you going to do?' I asked Colonel.

'Nothing,' came the reply.

'Betelgeuse, could I talk to Earth?' I asked.

'Of course.'

Colonel glowered.

I went to the communication console. 'Hello, Earth. Calling Earth, come in Earth, over,' I said. Then static. I tried again and again.

'Earth here. Who are you? Over,' came a very weak voice.

'Hello, Earth. This is Warboys from Redscout. Over.'

'Congratulations, we thought you'd had it.' There was a moment's silence.

'Warboys,' came the voice of the British Chief of Staff. 'What happened to Colonel Rhodes? Over.'

'He's here, but our ship was destroyed and we're now with the lead ship from the fleet that came in from heliocentric longitude 45°. I'd like permission for us to land in England. Over.'

'Our thanks to your rescue ship for saving the rest of our fleet. You have clearance to land. Over.'

'Thank you. Over and out.'

'Well, well, world control sounds happy for once,' said Colonel. 'I wonder if any of us know what we're in for.'

I stared hard at Betelgeuse. He looked back politely.

6

For an hour or more I watched Colonel wander purposefully around the cabin. It struck me as rather pigheaded of him not to accept the situation and try to work within his present confinement. Betelgeuse and his men, having set their ship's course, had left us alone in the main cabin and gone below to sleep.

'How did you know about the rescue signalling device?' Rhodes suddenly said, turning on me.

'I didn't know we had one. They told me.'

'What do you mean, "they told me"?'

'What I said. They picked it up and homed in on me,' I said, a little testily. I could see Colonel was unsure of me. 'Do you think they've got me brain-washed or programmed?' I asked.

'Dick, I'm uncertain of the whole situation. Here are these people who come out of nowhere, put an aggressor to flight and then return us to Earth. I feel that it isn't natural.'

'You may be quite right, but at this point in time we know that they have fast ships and can out-shoot us, but that they haven't tried to question us. Why don't we let them return us home and brain-wash some of our politicians rather than ourselves?'

'Maybe you're right,' Colonel said with a smile. 'But I'm still extremely suspicious of all this good will.'

'You should be. That's what you have been trained for. I'm suspicious too, but there are several points that need clearing up before I call them enemies. Why do they look exactly like us? They are rather big to withstand deceleration of continuous 3 g., which may mean they are technically far in advance of us, and it seems rather unnecessary to use a trick to find out landing procedure. Surely they could just call up the rest of their fleet and move in, instead of taking the lead ship to Earth, which, for Betelgeuse, could mean suicide.'

'That makes sense. Do you think we should sit tight?'

'Yes, and I suggest that, instead of landing at World H.Q., we go back to Mildenhall.'

'We can't do that!' he said.

'Why not? If your suspicions about Betelgeuse are correct, then all he'll get is the landing instructions for one base in England, not the complex landing instructions of World H.Q., which would be far more useful to him in the event of invasion.'

'Hm. I think it's a weak argument, but it would be rather a scoop if they were on our side,' Colonel said, warming to my idea. 'Yes, well, Betelgeuse will have to make something go wrong during the final descent.'

'I'm sure that can be arranged,' I said, looking round the cabin. 'Do you think their ships are much more advanced than ours?'

'By watching the way the ship is operated, I'd say they're quite advanced. The questions would be unending. What kind of propulsion do they have? How do they get such good movability in such a large ship?' Rhodes said, looking round. 'They have a superior artificial gravity device.'

'Simple questions to answer,' Betelgeuse said, coming out of the lift. 'We normally use what you'd call nuclear fission for power, but we switch over to Solar power if we are close enough to a bright star or sun. The improvements in manœuvrability have been made by doing away with manual control, except in emergencies, and computing tactical movements,' Betelgeuse said, going over to the control and lighting up a large map. We went over to join him. 'It is time to check the position of my fleet.'

'Why, are you worried that we might attack you?' Colonel said.

'Not at all. Your forces have been recalled out of the area, which is a wise decision.'

Colonel was silent. The expression on his face made me wonder whether he was feeling a little subdued at the thought that his ships were outclassed. It was a natural feeling for a military man.

'Are you expecting more trouble?' I asked, breaking the silence.

'Trouble for you, I think. If they get by my defences, they'll burn you up.'

'What! Set the Earth on fire?' I said.

'Not only the Earth, but everything surrounding it,' Betelgeuse said, with a hardness in his voice.

'Is that why you're here—to help us?' Colonel said.

77

'To warn Earth, not to protect Earth. I hope that my warning comes early enough, so that you can build space craft similar to this one and leave your homes. That's your only chance of survival.'

'That's ridiculous,' Colonel said.

'It may seem so, but we'll see.'

'But supposing you are right,' I said, 'how did this happen?'

Betelgeuse laughed. 'Well, for many years now we have been fighting a space war; and recently, over the past thirty years or so, alien space ships have appeared. You can imagine what was suspected. The Yela, who are one of the groups we are involved in fighting, thought that these ships were something to do with me. They apparently captured one, removed the crew, sent it back to its destination and followed it.'

'So they thought you were using our planet as a port of call,' I said, reflecting that it was probably what had happened to Tubby Fanshawe.

'Yes, a repair depot,' Betelgeuse said, interrupting my thoughts.

'Of course. Since the ship was crewed by people who looked like you, the deductions seemed so obviously true.'

'Quite. I think if you Earth people had had a different appearance, you'd have been fairly safe.'

'You remind me of the Flying Dutchman,' I said.

Betelgeuse looked puzzled.

'The Flying Dutchman sailed the seas of the Earth,

but could never land. You sail the seas of space,' I said, feeling my remark had gone very flat.

'That's all very well, Dick, but how does the Yela burn up a planet?' Colonel asked.

'By manipulation of the Earth's atmosphere,' Betelgeuse said.

'Is that possible?' Colonel said with dismay.

'For the Yela, yes.' Betelgeuse was interrupted by a voice on the intercom.

'We are nearing Earth.'

'What are our landing instructions?' Betelgeuse said.

'Well,' Colonel looked at me for a moment, 'Dick and I have decided not to take you to our main Earth space centre, but to return to my own headquarters.'

'So we can't learn too much about your landing instructions,' Betelgeuse said, laughing.

I felt the blood rush to my face.

'Yes, but there is possibly another valid point,' Colonel said, trying to cover up the embarrassment. 'You will be interrogated. At home we can put a good word in for you, but we couldn't guarantee this from the World Security fellows.'

This point hadn't crossed my mind; it sounded quite reasonable.

'You haven't time to worry about us, you must start building ships,' Betelgeuse said with feeling.

'I understand that, but you will still have to explain it to our political leaders.'

'All right. What do we do now?' Betelgeuse asked.

'Have you got any maps of the Earth?'

A moment or so later a large map appeared on a panel, and at the same time the lift doors opened and the rest of the crew appeared.

'World Space H.Q. is here at longitude 28°, latitude 39°. The homing wave length is 26.705 metres. Now, we really want to come down here at longitude 0°30', latitude 52°20'. The homing wave length is 20.96 metres.'

'I understand, so you want me to cut from one wave length to the other before landing,' Betelgeuse said, with a smile.

Rigel and the crew began to make preparations and within a second or two the sound of the homing bleep filled the cabin.

'How long will it take?' I asked.

'Not long. We will give your Earth people a show of aerobatics,' Rigel said.

'What do you do about deceleration pressure?' Colonel asked, obviously looking round for something to lie on.

'Oh, you have nothing to worry about. The cabin has counter gravitation to allow normal movement up to 10 g. Beyond that it is advisable to use couches,' Betelgeuse said with pride.

'Fine. What do you do about living accommodation?' Colonel asked.

'That is all below this cabin. When it is possible I'll show you round.'

'Would you like to hear your Space Control?' Rigel asked.

Colonel nodded. Rigel turned up the sound and we heard an American voice giving instructions for our arrival. Then suddenly: 'My God. The ship's out of control. Hello, hello, calling all space controls monitoring space craft. Possibility of crash landing, repeat, possibility of crash landing.' The replies and questions to his message came in from all over the world.

Betelgeuse had turned on one of the tele-cine cameras, which showed the Earth and our approach. It became bigger and bigger until we seemed to be right on top of the south-eastern part of England. We saw towns, trees, animals grazing and then—nothing.

'We are down,' Betelgeuse announced.

'Incredible landing,' Colonel said, obviously not believing it.

Colonel, Betelgeuse and myself descended in the lift. At last, terra firma. It was a marvellous sight. Unfortunately, my legs began to feel spongy and I sank in a very undignified way on to the ground.

'Hey, what's the matter, Dick?' Colonel asked.

'Nothing a night's sleep wouldn't put right,' I said, listening to running footsteps. Betelgeuse went back into the ship, and eventually returned with a small box.

'I think I might need a translator,' he said.

The security fellows arrived all out of breath. Their faces reflected the emotions that probably were being experienced by everyone on the base—fear, excitement and curiosity at the arrival of an alien space ship.

'Colonel Rhodes?'

'Yes, sergeant.'

81

'My instructions are to take you to security to await . . .'

'In London?' Colonel cut in.

'Yes, sir.'

'Well, Dr Warboys here is very tired. I will make his excuses. So run him back to Cambridge.'

'Well . . .'

'That's an order, sergeant.'

'Yes, sir.'

'Dick, you go off home and get some rest. If there is a scene from security, I'll fend them off. You've had a strenuous trip.'

'What about you?' I asked.

'I think we are a little more used to it,' Colonel said, looking at Betelgeuse.

'What about the ship?' I asked again.

'That'll be under heavy guard, sir,' said the soldier.

'Betelgeuse, are you . . . ?'

'It's all right,' Betelgeuse interrupted. 'My crew will wait until I return. If, however, I don't, their instructions are to leave Earth and take our fleet out of your Solar System.'

'Good,' I laughed. 'You're right to be suspicious.'

Betelgeuse handed me some capsules. 'Take one if you feel the balance in your ears is upset. They will bring it back to the normal state.'

The three of them moved off, to a helicopter that had just arrived. I waved a feeble goodbye and staggered towards the terminal. A couple of soldiers were on their way towards me, arriving just in time before I collapsed again. They carried me like a sack of potatoes and placed me with care in another helicopter.

'Thanks,' I said.

'Our pleasure,' smiled one of the young soldiers as he got in and took over the controls.

We rose high over the space craft and set off in the direction of Cambridge.

'What's the time?' I asked.

'19.05, sir.'

I reset my watch. It didn't seem to want to go, so I took it off and shook it vigorously. Nothing happened.

'Should think your batteries are dead,' came the observation. 'I've got a spare if you would like one.'

Opening the watch revealed nothing. I took out the miniature heat battery and shorted it across my tongue. 'I think you're right,' I said. I had felt no tingling. Changing the battery, I cleaned a speck of fluff from the transistor, and then closed the watch up and put it back on my wrist.

'Here we are, sir,' said the soldier. Looking out of the cockpit I could see King's College Chapel below.

'Can you put me down over there by the old tennis courts.'

The helicopter settled gently on St John's grass tennis courts. If the head gardener had seen this he'd probably have shot me with his evil smelling insecticide.

The soldier didn't leave straightaway, just in case I crumpled up again. My mind was almost blank. The thought of a good wholesome steak filled the blankness as I walked unsteadily into the college buildings.

'Good evening, Dr Warboys,' said the voice of the head porter as I tried to slip unnoticed to my rooms.

'Good evening,' I replied, longing to hurry on.

'A Colonel Ganges telephoned,' he said, falling into step beside me. 'And gave me instructions to see that you were well fed.'

I thanked him.

Once inside my room, I locked the door, flicked the TV on and went into the kitchenette to find the material of a substantial meal set on a tray. I opened the oven; it smelt delicious. A bottle of the College's best claret was already airing. Pleasurable anticipation swept most of my fatigue away.

Within five minutes I was sitting in front of the TV.

'Good evening,' said the announcer. 'All twenty-eight channels will now be showing a special political broadcast.' The Prime Minister's face appeared on the screen. No choice, I thought; he's got all the channels. I tucked into my supper with relish as I watched with a jaundiced eye.

'Good evening,' said the Prime Minister. 'As all of you are fully aware what has been happening during the last week, I do not think you will wish me to mince matters. The Solar System has been invaded by a powerful alien fleet of—ah hm—space ships. Who, or what these aliens may have been is unknown to us. Why the attack was prosecuted so fiercely, so relentlessly, is unknown to us. From whence the aliens came we do not know.'

How can he say things like that, I thought as he went on:

'For two days' duration, a fierce battle has raged in the vast spaces surrounding our Earth. The outcome has been a complete victory for the brilliantly controlled forces of the World Space Fleet. The unprovoked, unsought attack is over. Our bitter, hostile, implacable enemy, has retreated beyond the confines of the Solar System, his fleet shattered and broken.'

'You wait until the papers print the real story in the morning,' I said to the TV, but the Prime Minister just went on.

'My purpose tonight is to inform you of a further most remarkable circumstance—that near the end of the battle our World Fleet was joined by a second fleet, from outside our Solar System. This second fleet appears to be just as friendlily disposed to us, as the first was hostile. You will therefore realize that no cause for alarm exists when I say that—a—ha, hm—a ship of this second fleet has landed on Earth. Why it has entered the regions of the Solar System and from whence it came will shortly be known.

'I wish to conclude this announcement with an appeal. These are exciting times—the wind of change blows unceasingly. But I need hardly say that a vast gulf exists—between a justifiable pride and excitement in the achievements of our species—and the hysteria of unbridled curiosity. I therefore trust, and the government behind me trusts, that during the next few days no unseemly demonstrations will take place here in Britain

—whatsoever may happen in the—ah, hm—rest of the world.'

I listened to the speech with amazement and amusement. The information given was such a distortion of the truth; but then politicians had their own ways of leading the people along. It might not appeal to me, but it seemed to work.

The Prime Minister's smiling face vanished from the screen and back came the newscaster.

'After that important statement from the Prime Minister, we are now being joined by a world wide span of stations, including CBS and UBC of the United States of America, VDKA of Asia and the fraternal network of Africa. Our Master of Ceremonies for tonight is the distinguished American commentator, Dave Swan Vespa,' said the newscaster enthusiastically. The voices faded as I drifted into deep sleep.

The buzz of the door bell woke me. I peered blearily through a small magic eye which allowed me to see who was standing there. It was Sir John Fielding.

'Come in, Sir John,' I said, opening the door.

'Hello, Dick. How are the space legs?'

'Rather badly fitted to my misused body, but never mind. Sit down,' I said, moving my supper tray into the kitchen and switching off the television set. 'Can I get you a drink?'

'Thank you. I'll have a whisky and soda if you've got it.'

'What time is it?' I asked, as I made two drinks.

'About midnight. Thank you,' Sir John said, taking the drink I handed him.

'No wonder I'm stiff, sleeping in a chair for so long,' I said. 'Well, you look very thoughtful.'

'I am, Dick. I've been up in London listening to Colonel Rhodes and this fellow Betelgeuse.'

'Do you believe that Betelgeuse is for us, not against us?' I asked.

'We all have to, whether we like it or not. We have no way of proving him wrong, and he hasn't done anything that could be classed as a hostility.'

'What about this invasion business?'

'Again, very difficult to say. He holds all the interesting answers. What I'd like to know at this moment is what are the odds of humanoid creatures living in Ursa Major?'

'Pretty remote, I would have thought,' I said.

'Yes, well it's questions like that which I should like answered at the moment instead of getting information on technical achievements.'

'Well, apart from your curiosity, what's happening?'

'To start with, the Government has gone mad. Betelgeuse offered them the blueprints of his space ships, and they were all over themselves to study them. The people at the Ministry of Defence are so excited about them that they don't really take this Yela threat seriously.'

'I suppose as long as they're all happy, we'll be left in peace,' I said.

'Certainly, but the Americans, Russians, French and

practically everybody else are hopping mad that the ship came down in England, and that we had the first offer of the blueprints. I suppose the Government will now start playing politics,' Sir John said thoughtfully.

'I wouldn't worry,' I said cheerfully.

'But I do worry. Betelgeuse's story was quite convincing, and I think he was very disappointed at the way it was treated.'

'They didn't keep him in London then?' I said.

'No, he and Colonel Rhodes went back to Mildenhall. I believe Rhodes is going to look after Betelgeuse and the ship.'

'Did Betelgeuse give any reason for this space invasion apart from the fact that you were sending ships into a war?' I asked.

'Oh, yes. Have you got a chart of the galaxy?'

'Certainly,' I said, going over to my desk. Under a mass of papers I found my old chart, which looked rather rat eared. 'Is this any good?' I said, spreading it out.

'Fine. Now we are here, all right,' said Sir John pointing. 'Apparently in all these various areas there are different creatures living.'

I nodded.

'These creatures are completely different from us, and different from one another as well,' Sir John said.

'Well, which is the enemy? The people who fought us in the battle?'

'The ones who can withstand deceleration at 3 g.?' Sir John mused. 'They're apparently called Essans. They live here,' he said prodding the map, 'but they're only part of a big federation.'

'What sort of federation?'

'The whole lot, as far as I can gather,' Sir John said, moving his hand freely round the chart.

'What about Betelgeuse, then? Where does he come from?'

'He has no fixed base. His fleet cruises round the galaxy the whole time. All the others are against him; and unfortunately since the DSP 15 they're now against us. So the Government in a half-hearted way has suggested a pact between the Earth and Betelgeuse.'

'Idiots,' I said. 'The politicians are always involving themselves in other people's problems. You know I'm glad I'm not a politician. I'd be in an asylum.'

'Apparently,' Sir John went on, 'Betelgeuse is only afraid of some creatures called the Yela. Yela means "unseen ones". No one has ever seen them, hence the name.'

'Did he say anything about the Yela being able to set planets on fire?'

'Yes. That is one of the other questions I would have liked answered.'

The telephone buzzed. I didn't really want to answer it, but Sir John was obviously curious. I flicked the switch. Colonel Rhodes came up on the screen.

'Sorry to bother you, Dick, but one thing that Betelgeuse didn't tell us was that he'd captured one of these Essans.'

'Really, where is it?' I asked.

'Here in the ship. I thought I'd let you know just in case you're interested.'

'I am indeed.'

'Come over. I'll meet you here at the terminal and we can get frightened together,' Colonel said, with a laugh.

Sir John nodded.

'O.K., Colonel. I'll be coming over with Sir John Fielding.'

'Don't be too long,' Colonel said excitedly. The picture faded. I flicked the switch and turned to Sir John.

'I shan't be a moment,' I said and nipped smartly into the bedroom and changed into clean clothes.

Sir John was folding up the chart when I came back.

'Good,' Sir John said, opening the front door. We were both quite excited as we moved towards the helicopter parked in what had been the college car park.

'It should be interesting to see a creature that can withstand 3 g. deceleration for long periods of time,' I said.

Sir John slipped the instruction card in and a few seconds later we were on the move.

'I'm interested that Betelgeuse's ship is more advanced than the Essans',' Sir John said.

'I suppose that's the right way round. If you wander around the galaxy staying alive with no fixed home, then your technology would have to be much better than that of your enemies who have home bases.'

'Hmm.'

The helicopter made off away from the lights of Cambridge, and then up ahead I could see the high-powered lights of the space drome. We travelled quickly and it wasn't many minutes before we were landing on the tarmac outside the terminal building.

We left our machine and made our way to meet Colonel, who was propped up against the bar with a drink. On seeing us he downed it and moved towards us.

'Hello, Sir John, Dick,' he said.

'Tell me, why didn't Betelgeuse tell us about this prisoner?' asked Sir John.

'He didn't think it was that important, until I started questioning him about the Essans. At this point he simply said he'd got one on board,' replied Colonel with a smile.

We walked out of the terminal and across the concrete. The foreign ship looked sinister against the arc-lights.

The airlock doors were open, so we just walked in. I pushed a button for the lift, which took a moment or two to arrive. Sir John looked around him with interest. There was no real comparison between the DSP 15 and this ship.

Betelgeuse, Rigel and Alcyone were in the main cabin when we emerged from the lift.

Betelgeuse switched the translator on—he said, 'Good, you have come.'

'We're rather curious about this Essan you have,' Sir John said enthusiastically.

'I understand that,' Betelgeuse said with a twinkle in

his eye. Alcyone moved past us and vanished in the lift.

'I hope that your people are going to take the problem of evacuating the Earth seriously.'

'I'm afraid we'll have to wait and see. They're not so rational as yourselves and until they can see, feel or hear this threat, they will look upon your information rather warily, I'm afraid,' said Sir John.

'And you, Sir John. What do you think?' asked Betelgeuse.

'What can I say. Your account of the galactic war convinces me the situation is very serious, but I'm not sure that the answer is to evacuate,' said Sir John. He saw the look on the other's face and added: 'Maybe I am being illogical myself.'

Alcyone reappeared from the lift with the Essan in tow. For a second or so we just stared at the creature and then laughed with relief. It was squat and badger-like, but with a round gentle face. A timid roly-poly animal looking more like a cuddly toy than a fearsome enemy.

'Betelgeuse, you mean to tell us that these creatures were attacking our fleet?' Colonel said.

'Yes, this is one of them.'

The Essan looked absolutely terrified.

'What's your name?' asked Sir John.

Alcyone spoke for it.

'Ungnee,' came a lovely singing voice.

'Are you frightened of Betelgeuse?' I asked.

Alcyone translated.

'Of nearly everything,' said the Essan.

92

'But why?' I asked.

'Because the Essans are peaceful people. They lived on a wonderful planet. One day the enemy appeared and a terrific battle took place. The Essans lost and were taken into slavery,' said Betelgeuse.

'Amazing. Absolutely amazing,' said Sir John.

'It is no different from the history of Earth. Many times peaceful nations have been conquered by aggressors and forced into servitude, or made to serve as unwilling soldiers.'

'That's true,' said Colonel.

'Sir,' said Rigel.

'Yes. What is it?'

Betelgeuse took his earphones and listened. Then, over the intercom began to come a weird sound, almost musical. Ungnee was really frightened now, and tried to hide behind Alcyone. The musical sound became more intense. Betelgeuse had a very worried look on his face, and he signalled Alcyone to remove the Essan, which she did.

The musical sound began to turn into an electronic voice with fast dot-dash notations. Betelgeuse looked at us in despair. I didn't understand at first. The fast dot-dash notation seemed meaningless, then suddenly I heard it.

'This is the Yela—this is the Yela.'

A cold, uncontrollable shiver went straight down my spine. Anyone not believing Betelgeuse's story must surely be convinced. I looked at my colleagues. They didn't say anything, but stood motionless, listening.

7

We were still transfixed when Ganges appeared from the lift with Alcyone, followed by a large tweedy woman.

'Hello, Sir John, Betelgeuse, Warboys,' he nodded to each in turn. 'Got a mass of instructions from the higher brass, start with the lady—Miss Atlanta Belpuize.' He introduced us all. 'Anthropologist, you know —dam' clever—wants to compare you with us and all that sort of thing.'

Betelgeuse said courteously, 'We shall be pleased to give you whatever information you need.'

Atlanta Belpuize looked at him thunderstruck. 'Please open your mouth again,' she said. Betelgeuse did so. 'It's unbelievable,' she said. 'The dentition is identical with our own. I don't know what to think. I need a more detailed examination, but at first sight these are humanoids.'

'Just what I thought, dear lady,' said Ganges. 'But then I'm just a simple chap.'

'But, Ganges,' she said, 'the point is that the chances of this degree of similarity are extremely small'; she was excited and bewildered. 'I'd better get straight into this.' She picked up Betelgeuse's hand and began examining the fingers and joints minutely.

'Er—Miss Belpuize, could you take one of the others to pieces?' said Ganges. 'Top brass want to confer with Betelgeuse.' He extracted Betelgeuse from her clutches saying: 'Perhaps another member of the crew?'

Betelgeuse was about to speak when Atlanta Belpuize said:

'Want the girl of course and how about that er—hm—man over there?'

Rigel tried to look inconspicuous but everyone's attention was diverted by the irruption of the 3 M's. Spotting Ganges, they all grinned broadly.

'Come on, Betelgeuse,' said Ganges hurriedly. 'Got a lot to do.'

'Bad show, what!' the 3 M's said as one man.

'Dam' impertinence,' rapped Ganges, his red face suffused with anger, blue eyes popping.

'Not cricket, what!' chorused the 3 M's.

Ganges turned an outraged back on the company and only Alcyone saw the twinkle in his eye. She crossed to Betelgeuse and spoke to him quietly; he nodded, turned to the 3 M's and spoke in their own tongue. Their chortles died down and looks of dismay crossed the normally cheerful, open faces. They expostulated; Betelgeuse silenced them with a gesture and, turning to Atlanta Belpuize, said:

'The 3 M's will be very pleased to co-operate in any way you require. Alcyone will see that all our facilities are at your disposal.'

Sir John, Betelgeuse, Warboys and Ganges entered the lift. As the doors closed they heard the 3 M's muted explosion 'Gallfinders!'

'That,' said Sir John, 'sounds like disgust in any language.'

'Quite incapable of translation,' said Betelgeuse blandly. 'I hope Colonel Ganges is not too offended by their high spirits.'

'Hmph—whippersnappers,' said Ganges, 'still—like a bit of spirit—look after myself anyhow—think the Belpuize has her work cut out though.' The thought did not displease him.

I did not take much notice of the exchange as my mind was racing over what Betelgeuse had said in the ship. The sinister message of the Yela had put a sharp edge on my fear. I looked at Sir John; he was gravely preoccupied.

'I wonder what Miss Atlanta Belpuize would think of the Essan?' said Betelgeuse to Sir John. 'Perhaps that would be the kind of surprise she would be expecting,' Sir John smiled agreement.

'Essan?' said Ganges, as the lift stopped. 'What's that?'

Sir John explained about the prisoner.

'Hmm. Don't want to be stuffy,' said Ganges, looking very stuffy indeed, 'but security is my job you know. Responsible for Mildenhall, can't have private gaols in my own parish as it were! Let's have it out and I'll clap it in the cells.'

97

'As you wish,' said Betelgeuse. He spoke into the intercom.

Ganges called over some of his M.P.'s 'Got an alien prisoner,' he said. 'Can't risk a slip up, keep on your toes.' As he spoke Betelgeuse approached from behind him with the nervous Ungnee. The sergeant-major of Military Police looked over Ganges' shoulder, nothing showed on his face.

'Should we use shackles, sir?'

Ganges spun on his heel, his jaw dropped. ''Pon my soul,' he said in confusion. He turned to the sergeant-major, pulled himself together and, with a glare that would have blistered paint, growled, 'I'll see you in my office, sergeant-major.'

The leathery face of the N.C.O. remained impassive. 'Sir!' he said smartly.

'Wait a moment,' said Ganges.

He rejoined the three of us. 'It's not my day,' he said. 'Galactic skirmishes, top brass on my neck, big flap here, Atlanta Belpuize and now this.' He glowered at the diminutive Essan who had stopped shaking and was gazing spellbound up at the big red face.

'Dammit,' said Ganges. 'Looks as menacing as a guinea pig.'

Ungnee's small face registered serene pleasure.

'Hmph,' said Ganges, 'can't have a squad of big strong chaps standing guard, armed to the teeth, over this. Anyway,' he continued, 'Sir John has to take our friend to the Ministry, you, young Warboys, have a meeting with the technical boys to get that valve of

98

yours in production and installed in our ships. I've set them up in the lab here, where they are going through the papers you left here before your trip. They are making headway, but need a bit of help—boffins, hmph.' He turned to Ungnee. 'Come on, prisoner,' he said, 'quick march.' He made a gesture to the Essan to accompany him and walked back to the escort.

To my huge delight, well shared by the soldiers, Ungnee slipped his hand into the Colonel's and gambolled along fluting away in his musical voice. Even the back of Ganges' neck looked embarrassed.

'Get fell in,' roared the sergeant-major. 'Jump to it, Smith. What's the matter with you, Robinson!'

They formed a box round the Colonel and marched smartly off to the H.Q. building.

'Well,' said Sir John. 'He may give me the pip but . . .'

'He has a quality,' said Betelgeuse. 'Dr Warboys, Rigel will join you at your meeting; your valve can be useful to us too.'

Betelgeuse and Sir John set off for London and I went to the labs, once more immersed in the threat of the Yela.

In an hour or so we'd overcome the problems that had arisen. Production space and men had been organized. Rhodes had dovetailed his servicing squads into the system so that there could be no delay on installation. Rigel had joined us as promised and the co-operation had been fruitful; he had a massive knowledge of the physical science, much of it a long way in advance of our own. It was flattering and stimulating to find, however, that some of my ideas were new ground for him and on my way home I wished that the situation were different and could allow us time to co-operate on some of the most interesting fields.

I was dog tired and got into bed without delay, falling asleep straight away. I must have slept restlessly for when I woke in the morning my pillows were against the far wall. My books, watch and other articles including the electronic alarm were scattered all over the room.

The door buzzer was going like mad and, feeling foul, I pressed the intercom button.

'Yes.'

'Good morning, Dick,' came Sir John's voice. 'Sorry to disturb you.'

'O.K. I'm coming,' I said, slipping on my dressing-gown. I opened the door. 'Come in.'

'I've brought a friend for you to look after for the day,' Sir John said briskly. Behind him stood a rather shy Alcyone. She'd discarded her green uniform and was dressed in a blue-green jacket and trousers.

'Good morning,' I said, a little embarrassed at my bare feet.

Alcyone laughed gently. She'd seen my quick glance at my feet. 'Good morning, Dick.'

'Well, I'll leave you. I shall be at the War Office; there is a lot to do. I'm glad your end is tied up, and a day off would do you good,' Sir John said, making his way towards the staircase.

'Come in, Alcyone,' I said, waving a farewell to Sir John.

Alcyone entered diffidently, but once she saw the general untidiness her step became more lively. She wandered around, and then made her way to the window. I must admit the view was one of the best in the university with the old chimney pots and roofs and in the distance the delicate spires of King's College chapel. A view that's probably remained much unchanged for five hundred years.

'You haven't got a translator,' I said, covering my bare feet.

'No. One of my jobs is to learn languages. When we rescued you, I had time to run a programme on the English language, and then I started to learn. Betelgeuse and the others are learning too.'

'But your command of the language is extremely good for a few hours; what did you do, plug yourself into the computer?'

'Something like that,' she laughed gently.

'Laugh you may; how about applying your advanced knowledge to making a cup of tea.'

'A cup of tea, is that a drink?'

'Yes.'

'Well, I can try.'

I went back into the bedroom and tidied up, showered, shaved, dressed and hurried back to see what Alcyone was up to. She sat in the kitchen engrossed in an old cookery book, that my great-great-grandmother had used.

'Quite an interesting document,' she said, looking at a recipe for Christmas pudding.

I looked round. 'No tea?'

'Ph, I'd forgotten,' Alcyone said.

I found a couple of mugs that weren't damaged in one way or another and put tea tablets in, poured on some hot water and threw a couple of milk pills in for luck.

'You don't make tea like that,' she said.

'Don't you?' I handed one of the mugs to Alcyone.

'How to make tea,' Alcyone said, pointing to the recipe book. 'Boil a kettle of water. Pour a little boiling water into a teapot and allow pot to warm. Throw the water away and add three spoons of tea and pour on boiling water. I don't really understand it.'

I laughed. 'It's very simple really, and occasionally, when I can get tea leaves, I make it that way. I'll show you some time.'

Alcyone put the book down and looked at me thoughtfully.

'I will tell you one of the most remarkable things about you, and many people I've met on Earth,' she said, sipping her tea.

'Go on.'

'Well, you believe there will always be a tomorrow. Whatever the disasters, the days will pass and time will heal all wounds or at least the surface of these wounds,' she said.

'Well, why not?'

'Do you believe that there really is a tomorrow?'

'Personally I believe in a tomorrow. Sometimes I have doubts about next year, but it doesn't last.'

'You realize that there is no real tomorrow for us?'

'Oh, come off it. You'll be here tomorrow.'

'You don't understand. Soon there will be a great grief for all you Earth people.'

'I understand that we were attacked the other day, and we might be attacked again in the future, but I can enjoy today.'

'But it won't be the same sort of attack. The next time the Yela itself will come. It may be soon, it may be many years, but the Yela will come—and then there will be death, everywhere, all over the face of the Earth.'

'But how will the Yela produce such devastation?'

'Perhaps you will realize how when I say that the Yela are capable of moving a blanket of hydrogen around a planet.'

'How much gas?'

'As much as is in the atmosphere of the planet itself.'

'Then these Yela people do have tremendous powers,' I said, getting up.

'Yes. They don't move hurriedly. A planet is slowly surrounded with hydrogen, so that below is the oxygen of the ordinary atmosphere and above is the hydrogen blanket. Then at one place the hydrogen is pressed in.'

'Good Lord!' I said, beginning to visualize the terrifying picture.

'You begin to see? The hydrogen and oxygen combine with a great release of heat. The heat causes the gas to rise and more hydrogen is sucked down. Within a few minutes the whole atmosphere everywhere—is a raging inferno.'

'Quite a bomb. Makes a nuclear weapon seem like a pop gun.' I walked over to the window. 'How did it happen to you?' I turned to face Alcyone.

'Well,' Alcyone said, getting up and coming over to join me. 'About a hundred thousand years ago, we began spreading our people from planet to planet— Mankind, the human species. We moved steadily from one star to the next. We thought of ourselves as masters of the galaxy. At one time, many, many thousands of planets were under our control.'

'Then this expansion, I suppose, came to an end?'

'Yes, after an attempt to invade the territory of the Yela, we were vigorously repulsed. Then the Essans joined with many other oppressed creatures and allied against us, resulting in a long war.'

'Did you lose?' I asked, treading carefully.

'Not immediately. We were winning, when the federation appealed to the Yela for help. The Yela decided against us—from then on it wasn't really a war any more—only continuous disasters.'

'So you had to keep moving, I suppose. Never landing at any place for more than a little while,' I said.

'That's right. Except on one planet, one fluke planet —the Earth.'

'The Earth! Why particularly the Earth?' I asked.

'Because here, by a million to one chance, there

104

happened to be primitive men—creatures resembling ourselves.'

'That would be Neanderthal man,' I said thoughtfully to myself.

'Yes, that's right,' Alcyone said, catching my remark.

'So you think a few of your survivors managed to land here. Intermingled with the true inhabitants, and used them as a sort of camouflage?'

'Yes, that's exactly what happened. Now you understand why we look alike.'

'Indeed I do, but it's a weird story.'

'Yes, and to make matters worse, in time you Earth men developed space craft and went exploring. A foolish mistake, for then it was known outside your solar system that humans inhabited the Earth. You were not to know this, but the damage is done. The Yela will come.'

'Yes, but why are you so sure we're helpless?'

'We've tried everything. Your only chance is to build ships like ours and escape with us.'

'I don't see that that's the only answer. Surely we might try to argue some sort of case. After all, it's fifty thousand years since this happened.'

'Ah, yes. Fifty thousand years ago when we landed here, the Earth was teeming with animals. Today all the primitive men are extinct and many species of animals. Your domination, to the Yela, is a form of oppression. A fine case you'll be able to argue,' Alcyone said with feeling.

The sun was beginning to come through from behind

a large bank of grey clouds. It didn't seem possible, looking out over the roofs and chimneys, that somewhere out in the bluey-black depths of space was a fearsome, relentless enemy.

'You look thoughtful,' Alcyone said, taking my arm.

'I am indeed! Still, let's go out for a bit,' I said.

'Don't you ever learn?' Alcyone cried in despair.

'Certainly, but only under severe pressure,' I said, going over to my desk. I found my pass book and credit cards. 'Where would you like to go?' I asked, tucking them into my pocket.

'Somewhere that you would like to go.'

'Fine, come on then.'

I closed the door and stuck up a note. OUT FOR THE DAY. Then I had second thoughts and added a footnote saying that my message taker was switched on. A very simple device. The front-door bell works on body temperature, so that the visitor stands for a moment until his body heat is picked up by a heat cell, then the buzzer goes. I'd put this in one day when I had nothing better to do, because people complained I was never in and lost notes and messages. When the buzzer goes it turns the tape machine on and the visitor just speaks into the intercom microphone in the door.

We walked through the old part of the college. Alcyone was very quiet and looked a little wistful at the sight of all the old buildings. I wondered if they stirred some ancient memory in her. At the main gate, I asked one of the porters to hire me a helicopter.

Five minutes of slow walking brought us to the old

market square, where we were to pick up the helicopter. It is strange how tradition carries on, I thought. The Cambridge market was in full swing, with its wooden stalls covered in gaily coloured fabric to keep rain and sun off the goods. Some of the stalls we passed were stacked high with potatoes, lettuce, fruit and flowers.

'It's fabulous,' Alcyone said, walking happily round a flower stall. 'I have only read and seen pictures of such things.'

We walked round the whole market several times before Alcyone would be dragged away. Funny, I thought to myself, as I followed her round. I'd been in Cambridge for over ten years and the market had never struck me as a rarity. We take many beautiful things for granted because they are familiar.

'How long do you think you'll be?' said the man with the helicopter.

'Oh. I'll keep it until tomorrow,' I said, handing over my credit card.

'Where are you going?' the man asked.

'Well, I thought I'd go over to the east coast.'

'I'll give you a stack of empty cards and you can punch them for yourself. There are some detailed maps in the front pocket.'

'Come on,' I said to Alcyone, who was engrossed by an argument over the price of some potatoes.

'Where are you going to take me?' she asked, getting in beside me.

'Well,' I said, taking a quick look at a map of the area, 'how about going to Dunwich.'

'What is this place, Dunwich?' Alcyone asked as I punched out the instructions on a card.

'It's a lovely old village by the sea.'

She looked at me as though I were mad. I pushed the instruction card into its slot and started up the motors. The day was now superb, a clear blue sky, warm sun and a vast patchwork of streets below us as we took off. We were whisked on to our course and were soon out over the green countryside. Newmarket came and went.

'No wonder you don't really worry. It's absolutely beautiful,' Alcyone said, smiling happily at the fields and woods below.

In a little over half an hour we were standing on soft yellow sand looking out over the green North sea. Dunwich was a strange village, left over from the seventeenth century. Despite all that modern technology could offer, this quaint village had slipped gently into the sea. Alcyone laughed when she saw the church which was sunk in the beach almost on the sea's edge. We walked over to it, and it made me think of a giant treasure chest buried in the sand at a strange angle.

'Why hasn't all this been demolished?' Alcyone said, looking at a shattered window.

'Possibly because we've destroyed so much in the past that people don't really care what happens any more.'

'You are all full of contradictions,' said Alcyone lightly. 'You care nothing of an invasion from outer space, and yet you care about an old subsiding church. You may say that you don't care about the church, but

I have a feeling it brings you and others a certain peace of mind.'

'You're probably right about it giving me peace of mind. I like the old world, the new one is a little too precarious for my peasant approach. Tell me, how do you keep sane?' I asked, trying to imagine what I would do floating through an endless universe.

'It is difficult. I suppose that knowing one will be safe from attack is the main thing. The more you think about it the worse it gets, and one begins to realize, as I do now, that all the time we live on our nerves.'

'What do you do though, get yourself immersed in the problems of this strange galactic war?' I said, making a move towards an old pub set back from the beach.

'You think it's strange for us to fight an endless war. I suppose it is hard to understand, but imagine yourself exiled. Not just sent away or driven out, but shot at, always hunted.'

'Yes. It's what we'd call guerilla warfare.'

'That was the word I was looking for,' Alcyone said, as I pushed open the door to the public bar.

'Where did these people come from?' she said in a whisper as we entered the bar. I saw why she was a little surprised. The silent staring eyes of a row of old men who had probably been sitting in the same place for the last fifty-odd years.

'It's all right, they're just suspicious of strangers, that's all,' I said.

'Good morning,' said a jolly red-faced man from behind the oak wood bar with its multitude of liquor stains.

'Good morning. One and a half pints of best bitter, please.'

Alcyone looked round at the low oak-beamed room. Relics from the past hung from the ceiling to the floor. We propped ourselves up against the bar. The stale smell of beer was very noticeable.

'Would you like something to eat?' I asked her. She shook her head.

'What have you got?' I said, turning back to the man behind the bar.

'Well, really depends on what you be wantin'.'

'Steak and kidney pie?' I said, hoping.

The man smiled, nodded, and vanished through a door behind the bar.

'If you don't like this, you can have something else,' I said, passing the half pint of beer to Alcyone. 'It's a very English drink.'

The landlord reappeared with a large pie on a dish. 'Like this, sir?'

'Genuine?' I said, savouring the beautiful aroma.

'Certainly. My wife's speciality.'

The pie tasted really good. I remembered my mother cooking pies like this for my father.

'Do you want a bit?'

'Yes,' said Alcyone taking a large mouthful. 'What is it?'

'A home-made steak and kidney pie,' I said, taking a sip of my beer.

'I wonder what these people think about the Yela,' Alcyone said, studying the weather-beaten faces.

'I'm not sure, but why don't you ask?'

'I can't. I would be too embarrassed.'

'Well,' I laughed. 'That's the only way you'll find out. Excuse me,' I asked one florid-faced man. 'This young lady would like to know what you think about the Earth being invaded.'

''hose goin' to invade 'arth?'

'I was just asking a theoretical question.'

'Yes, I heard there might be a possibility,' said the landlord. 'There was a battle out in Space a few days ago.'

'That's right. Well, what I want to know is, what you'd all do if we hadn't won?'

'Ah, well if 'hey come, then I'll carry on as usual,' said the florid-faced man.

'Just carry on!' Alcyone said in amazement.

'That'll be right, young lady,' said another man.

'But don't you realize what is going to happen?' she said.

'No, you tell us.'

'Well, when this hidden enemy strikes you'll all be killed.'

'That may be so, but 'em will 'ave to be cleverer than us.'

'Yes,' said the landlord. 'The other nations of the world may not do much, but we'll certainly go down fighting.'

'But you'll still die,' Alcyone said.

'Maybe, but not without taking some of them with us.'

'Does that give you some idea of what you're dealing with?' I said, finishing my drink.

'But I don't really understand the thinking behind their attitude.'

'Here in England, I think it is a tradition rather than a logical approach. Many, many years ago we had two classic wars here in Europe, after which England became more and more financially embarrassed as time went on. The politicians tried first to join up with the Americans, and then with Europe to get us out of our difficulties. Then a bright politician realized that Britain might be in financial trouble, but we were still producing ideas, good ideas in technology. So instead of giving these ideas away as had happened in the past, because of lack of development money, the government pumped vast sums of money into technology.'

'Did it help?'

'Oh, yes. The British settled down as they had done during the two big wars and, while the rest of the world slowed down in technological advancement, we went ahead. Slowly the other countries started spending their money, not on technological ideas but on buying ours.'

'I see that you are very proud of this.'

'Of course, that is why there's always the possibility that we might find some way of frightening the Yela off,' I said with a certain amount of pomp.

'You are saying that the rest of the world may now be looking to England for an answer?'

'Possibly.'

'But what about the space ships?' Alcyone asked.

'You mean, yours?'

'Yes.'

'Well, I should think they'll build one from your blueprints. Not to escape from a burning Earth, but to help fight off any outside invasion.'

'But don't you realize there's nothing you can do?' Alcyone said crossly.

'There must be something. You shouldn't always think of defeat. We might be able to do something.'

'But you're not the first to fight their threat! Do you think ten thousand planets allowed themselves to be destroyed without attempting to fight?'

'Alcyone, let's not argue, it isn't getting us anywhere. If there's no chance of defeating this danger, then we'll humbly accept your knowledge, but first give us time to think,' I said, beginning to feel irritated at the barrage.

'You haven't time to think,' Alcyone said angrily.

I took hold of her hand and we made our way out of the pub. She was quiet as we walked back to the helicopter. It was sad that she wanted to go home, but I was growing angry, so it was probably just as well.

'Dick,' she said, as we reached the helicopter. 'I'm sorry to be cross with you, but my instinct of survival is maybe stronger than yours, and if you're not going to come with us, regardless of what other Earth people think, then I must leave you.'

'Alcyone, what are you trying to say?' I said, taking hold of her by the shoulders, so that she had to look into my face.

'We wanted you to come with us.'

'I don't understand. Why me? There are men of far greater stature and intellectual calibre.'

'No, it is not as complicated as that. Betelgeuse things that you are of value to me.'

'To you!' I exclaimed. 'But you've hardly seen me.'

'I like you though, and I wanted to save you.'

'I'm very flattered, but how can you be sure that I'm not a mean pig?' I said, looking at her. She was very pretty.

Alcyone laughed. 'I don't know, but I still think it worth getting to know you.'

I didn't know what to say. It was very flattering to be saved, but I couldn't see myself bottled up in a space ship, being subject to acceleration forces, confined spaces and endless time. I suppose if I'd my laboratory along with me, that would be better, but how long would it be before I felt fed up. The whole thing was out of proportion, I thought, if it was a question of trying to solve the problem and die in the attempt, I'd prefer that to living and dying in a space ship.

'Will you take me back?' Alcyone said.

'Certainly, but don't you want to see a little more of England?' I asked.

'I would like to, but you must make up your mind about coming with us. If I'm with you, you'll not take the situation seriously,' she said.

114

We reached the helicopter. I programmed it to take us to Alcyone's space craft. The flight was made in relative silence. When we arrived, the place was swarming with television technicians and their followers. The helicopter came to rest in the park.

'We'll have to make a run for it,' I said, looking at swarms of TV newscasters coming towards us.

'I think you're right,' Alcyone said, smiling for the first time.

'Excuse me, sir. Could you give us a word on the current situation?' A persistent reporter pushed his microphone at us.

'Sorry, we don't know what current situation you're talking about.'

'The galactic war,' said another.

Several large security guards manoeuvred the press and TV men away and escorted us to the space craft.

'Will you come and see us?' said Alcyone, about to enter the airlock.

'Certainly. Here's my phone number,' I said, handing her my phone card. 'I'll drop in some time during the week unless something urgent comes up.'

'You're going back to work?'

'I'm afraid so. I have a lot of work to catch up on.'

Alcyone smiled almost sadly and went in.

I fought my way back through the press and TV men and with a feeling of relief got the helicopter into the air.

8

I had plenty on my mind. The threat of the Yela occupied me constantly. Betelgeuse and his people were more advanced in technology than we were and they had not found a substantial defence. But since they were nearly always travelling through space, they were physically limited from developments that needed big stable resources. Rigel was in many ways ahead of me in his knowledge and yet he admitted that in my own field I had ideas new to him. Were his people too restricted by their life to break out of the Yela's grip? Could I help because I was not being inhibited by their environment? But how could one counter an attack when one was not sure of the way it would be launched? I had to see Sir John and Betelgeuse.

The Market Square was below. I landed and walked back to College deep in thought. Once in my room I rang Sir John. His image appeared on the screen.

'Hello, Sir John. I would like to see you about something important.'

'Good,' he said. 'I was just about to ring you. World H.Q. is worried by Betelgeuse's forces out in space.'

'Why?'

'I've no idea, but they're working like mad to get the

blueprints put into action,' Sir John said dryly. 'However, there is one interesting development.'

'Oh, what's that?'

'We've had more strange signals.'

'Did you get a tape?'

'Yes. Look, let's get a bite to eat while we play it,' Sir John said with a certain amount of enthusiasm.

'Fine, where?'

'What about Le Jardin, say in about half an hour,' Sir John said, looking at his watch.

I nodded and the screen went dead.

A little later I hailed a hover taxi.

'Where to, sir?'

'Le Jardin. The French restaurant on Hills Road,' I said.

The man pressed a button and the vehicle lifted off the ground. A slight sound came from the fan below me, but once it reached full operating speed, everything went quiet.

Sir John stood outside the restaurant, with a small portable tape recorder in his hand. I gave my credit card to the taxi man, who punched it and then gave it back to me, while I signed the receipt.

We turned to go into the restaurant. Sir John really revels in a little bit of convention. This particular restaurant was owned by the founder's grandson who, under great difficulties, had decided to go on running the restaurant with waiters and barmen, like those of the 1970s. All other eating places were now completely automatized, choice remaining only in the different ways of ordering one's food, and I suppose the decor came into it. For instance, the inexpensive cafés are very simple. You sit at a long table with a moving panel in the middle. Having chosen from the menu list, you punch your choice and the food comes up within seconds on the moving panel. In more expensive restaurants there are separate tables. A microphone is used to order food. According to the advertisements, this is the personalized way.

'Good evening, Sir John,' said Pierre, the proprietor. 'Your usual table?'

'Yes, Pierre, that would be very pleasant.'

We made our way through tightly packed tables, crowded with people.

'It's incredible,' I said, sitting down.

'What?'

'How many people seem to like the old sort of restaurants.'

'Yes, and the bulk of them are young people like yourself, Dick,' smiled Sir John.

'Maybe, but I'm a young person who feeds himself anywhere.'

Sir John looked exasperated at my statement and buried his head in the long menu.

'Would you care for a drink?' Pierre asked.

'Hm. Yes, I'll have a whisky and water. Dick?'

'A gin and tonic, please.'

Pierre marched off, nodding and smiling as he went. We concentrated on the menu.

Our drinks appeared. I took a good sip and then

turned to the waiter who was ready to take our orders.

'For you, sir?' he said.

'I'll have the Cordon Bleu steak, with a few sauté potatoes and a green salad,' I said, all in one breath.

'Steak, again!' Sir John murmured.

'Would you like anything to begin with?' asked the waiter.

'No thanks.'

'I'll have the duck in orange sauce, and a mixed salad,' Sir John said.

'Wine, sir?'

'How about rosé? Pierre has got some of the best I've tasted in years.'

'Fine by me.'

'We'll have a carafe of the Californian rosé,' said Sir John.

Once the waiter had gone, Sir John put the mini tape machine on the table and handed me an earphone.

I put the ear plug in, and Sir John flicked the switch on the tape recorder. The strange weird electronical music came through. I listened for a few minutes and then took the earpiece out.

'Has anyone deciphered what the Yela are trying to say?' I asked, pointing at the tape.

'Not really. The Jodrell Bank people say the sound seems to be coming from a fixed point, almost as if they were marshalling their forces.'

'Not a very good sign. Has anyone talked to Betelgeuse?' I asked.

'Yes, and he's going mad because nobody's taking it

seriously. According to him, they are working on hydrogen pushing.'

'Well, what's going to happen?' I asked.

Sir John shrugged his shoulders. 'How serious do you think things really are, Dick?'

'Very serious—but what infuriates me is that our visitors would rather we fled with them than stand and make a fight of it.'

'Is that what the girl told you?'

'Yes. She wanted me to go back to the ship and leave with them.'

'Oh,' Sir John said, chuckling as the waiter put our food on the table. 'Why didn't you accept the offer?'

'I don't really know. Perhaps the thought of giving up doesn't really appeal to me,' I said thoughtfully.

'But think of all that new technology you would be able to learn,' Sir John went on.

'I know, that had crossed my mind, but at the moment I feel there must be something we can do to stop the Yela, if we're really in earnest.'

'You feel you can fight a people who can burn a planet up?' smiled Sir John.

'Well, I know the Yela are further advanced in technology, but surely we can try to outwit them.'

'True, but even if you stop them once, they might come back a second time. Can we be sure to stop them again?'

'I don't know, but with a breathing space we might gain the confidence of Betelgeuse and make him believe that it is possible to fight calculated battles rather than just play guerilla warfare,' I said, taking a mouthful of steak.

'Do you think that Betelgeuse is really afraid of these Yela?' Sir John said.

'No, I don't think his people are afraid while they are in space. Their ships are as good or better than most of the federation fleet. Their main fear is of this burning phenomenon that the Yela can perform. So while they're on a planet a sense of despair sets in, which makes them believe that nothing can be done.'

'Maybe, maybe,' said Sir John, finishing his meal. 'What do you consider would be the best thing to do?'

I took a sip of wine and a deep breath. 'Try to deliver one blow, which would destroy enough of the enemy to make them retreat to lick their wounds.'

'How would you do that? It is obvious that our conventional weapons would be of very little use,' Sir John said thoughtfully.

'Yes, and extremely expensive. Colonel Rhodes tried an idea for making a batch of torpedoes hunt together. But this is such a waste, when you consider that with eight torpedoes you can only hit two ships.'

'So you want one or two torpedoes or some similar weapon that can tackle a fleet spread over a wide area. How about Quark torpedoes, or a giant Quark bomb?' said Sir John, fiddling with his spoon.

'A Quark bomb would be extremely interesting, but it wouldn't have enough heat value over a wide area,' I said, beginning to scribble some calculations down on my napkin.

Quarks had been a great joke until the end of 1969, when it was proven that the smallest known atom particles at the time could be split even further. The man who discovered this called these particles Quarks. This was quite a breakthrough, as the practical use showed that a Quark bomb was thousands of times more powerful than the conventional hydrogen one.

I looked up. 'No. It's as I thought, the heat intensity would be too low.'

'Even if you used Quark heads on torpedoes?' asked Sir John, finishing his wine.

'Could be, but I'm not satisfied with the idea.'

Pierre came up and placed a small TV set on the table. A picture of the Prime Minister came into focus.

'Good evening,' he said. 'As you will have heard from our experts, no serious importance need be attached to the—hm, rather singular interruptions that have been taking place recently in our broadcasts.'

I looked at Sir John, who shrugged his shoulders.

'Our enemy has been soundly, roundly defeated. Smarting no doubt under his defeat, he is now indulging in the childish pastime of vain threats. Nevertheless, World Space H.Q., with the full approval of all governments, proposes to take precautionary measures. During the next few days full-scale manœuvres are to be held. These will include a defence exercise in which the population as a whole will be expected to take part. Over the period of the operation, starting from midnight tomorrow, I would appreciate your full co-operation in observing all the regulations that will be given out as the exercise develops.'

'Idiots,' said Sir John getting up. 'Won't be a moment.' He vanished towards the phone booth. I emptied the remains of the wine carafe into my glass and drained it. Sir John came back to the table.

'Nobody's talking, and the War Department had the cheek to tell me to mind my own business.'

'Do you think they're going to put Betelgeuse's replica up and try to fight?' I said, almost laughing at my own question.

'Pierre,' Sir John bellowed.

'Yes, Sir John?'

'What else has been happening?' he said, pointing to the TV.

'I'm afraid I don't know. My wife saw there was going to be a broadcast so . . .'

'Fine, Pierre. Thank you, put the meal on my account.'

Pierre smiled nervously as Sir John swept out of the restaurant, with me following in his wake.

'Dick, I'm going home to see if I can learn anything more of what's going on.'

'Good idea,' I said. 'If there's anything I can do . . .'

'Yes, yes, thank you, Dick. I'll be in touch,' Sir John said absently and walked off in the direction of his home.

I turned and started to walk towards the city centre. Had World H.Q. suddenly decided to put more ships up, knowing that they'd be annihilated once they were within range of the enemy? They couldn't have more than one or two ships of the Betelgeuse type. I had to find out. I called up Colonel Rhodes.

It took ages to track him down, but eventually the central phone computer found him.

'Hello, Dick. How are the sea legs?' said Colonel when he came up on my small monitor.

'Not too bad. A little rubbery from time to time. Look, Colonel, I've just seen the Prime Minister on the box, and I was wondering what the devil he was talking about.'

'Perhaps I shouldn't be telling you over the open phone, but we've been put on security alert. According to Ganges' information, everyone's voted to have a go at the enemy using Quark torpedoes,' Rhodes said, looking rather tired, I thought.

'Won't do much good,' I said.

'I have the same feeling,' Rhodes said, guardedly.

'What's the chance of my coming over and talking to you and Betelgeuse?'

'Nil, the base is all closed up except for authorized personnel.'

'Couldn't you get me a pass?'

'Not at the moment. We've got a lot of top brass here; they've even put Betelgeuse and the crew under a sort of house arrest.'

'What happens if I turn up?' I asked.

'Nothing, you're quite respected round here; but as I said, there's pandemonium going on so nothing can be guaranteed.'

'O.K., Colonel, don't get yourself into trouble this time, I shan't be around,' I said, pulling the switch before Rhodes could get an answer in.

The situation annoyed me. I wanted to discuss with Betelgeuse an idea that was forming in my mind. The more I walked the stronger the feeling of anger grew. Eventually I'd made up my mind. I'd go and see him.

The problem was how. A helicopter or taxi was out of the question. I'd have to give the destination, which would give me away immediately. So how does one travel about twenty miles without walking?

The college library was still open when I got back. My head began to go like a fast metronome as I searched for a detailed six-inch to the mile map of the Mildenhall area. Marvellous, nobody had borrowed it. I looked round to see if anyone was watching. No, so I put the map in my pocket and went back to my rooms.

The problem was no easy one to solve. All means of transport gave the authorities and the police an account of my movements into the area. Another problem was, once in the vicinity of Mildenhall, I'd have the radar to deal with. This second question annoyed me, as I'd done a lot of work on it in my early days at the University. From what I knew, the equipment was becoming obsolete now, but it could still detect a moving object from almost ground level upwards.

I poured a gin and tonic and sat looking intently at the map. It was possible to reach the perimeter of the space drome, but then I would have to make a run for it, with the chance of being picked up within minutes by the security patrols.

It is strange that when you're thinking hard about a problem the solution can be so simple it is overlooked. I went to my desk and hunted through my files until I found a very tattered one marked 'RADAR'. I'd been painstakingly meticulous in the data. Here it was, a rough sketch of the ground radar plan. True, it would have been altered, but from what I could remember there were a number of aerial points. These were collapsible, and could be withdrawn into the ground. The electronics were fed through small tunnels from the control room.

There were several possibilities. Outside the perimeter there were eight aerial points. Two on the south side had tunnels running alongside the main launching pad area. I thought carefully and then put a cross at the approximate position of Betelgeuse's ship. There were no ventilation points for the tunnel marked near the ship but there must be one. There seemed to be no choice; if I wanted to go, I would have to do it this way.

It was starting to rain as I packed up a small tool kit and crept stealthily from my rooms. I wended my way through various courtyards until I reached the old kitchen bridge that crossed the river Cam. The senior tutor kept a small canoe moored here, mainly to get to and from his home, which was upstream. He would blow up when he found it gone, but it wouldn't harm him to walk. Being no boatman, my antics getting into the canoe must have been amusing. Once in it, it rocked so much I had to sit very still for fear of falling into the water. I slipped the mooring and the canoe slowly moved out into the river and started to drift downstream. I lay quietly in the bottom as it was still early enough for students to be out with their girlfriends, even though the rain was falling.

Suddenly the canoe picked up speed. This must be the lock. It was, and I was travelling at an ever-increasing speed towards it. It took me a few seconds to get everything under control, but luckily I made it, as there was a weir with a good fifteen- to twenty-foot drop to the lower part of the river.

I carried the canoe round the obstacle and soon found myself at the boat yard I was looking for. Here, as I suspected, were several hover water ski boats tied up along the jetty. Each one was connected up to a recharging unit. I tested every boat and then slipped the rope on the one with the most stored electricity. My plan was now simple. The river Cam led into a large river called the Ouse. There was, according to my map, a river called the Lark coming into the Ouse from the south-east. This would lead me to the south of the space drome.

The journey was uneventful, except for the fact that I kept running into odd things, as I didn't want to use the lights on the boat. The launching pads were lit up to look like daylight, and over towards the far end I could see the DSP 15 and, just beyond it, Betelgeuse's ship. There seemed to be a terrific amount of activity and the main carrying railways were crowded with ships ready to be put on the pads.

I moored the boat to the east end of the village of Mildenhall, which positioned me just to the south of the space drome. Lying on the river bank it took me several minutes to decide roughly where I was.

In my tool kit I'd put a small radio receiver which was capable of picking up ultra high frequency waves. It did the trick. I was almost sitting on one of the aerials. Crawling on my stomach, I eventually reached it, and just below was a manhole cover. I counted the time that the aerial was pointing away from me. Not much time; next time round I crawled quickly up to the manhole cover and pried it open. Below, all I could feel was cold water. I climbed in just as the aerial came round again. The water smelt foul as I sank into it. The tunnel holding the communications cables was flooded halfway up the wall.

My map of the tunnels was beginning to get rather damp and flabby. I found my compass and placed it on the disintegrating paper and shone my pocket light. If I was right about the position of the aerial, all I had to do was to take the first tunnel east and then the second going north.

With one leg and arm astride the communications cable I started to crawl along the tunnel. The water was cold, muddy and strangely wet. I crawled and crawled, and I began to feel as though I'd crawled all the way back to Cambridge before I came to my turn to the east. Suddenly the ground shook and a deafening roar shook me to the core. The whole tunnel seemed to flex. I must be under a launching pad. I wiggled my head around when it was over and started moving again, as the cold of the water was beginning to creep into my bones. One tunnel was past and then shortly I arrived at my turning north. At this point I consulted my chart. I tried to picture what was above me, but it was difficult. I moved on a little until I found a gridded manhole cover. No amount of physical strength would move the grate, but I could see and hear terrific activity. They were launching craft as fast as they could.

As I crawled on, another ship went up and the tunnel flexed alarmingly. Eventually I arrived at the next cover. This one must have been nearly twenty feet below ground level, so I had to climb up a small ladder. Heaving away at the cover didn't seem to have much effect. I looked at the edges; there didn't seem to be any locking device, but peering through the slits I saw a pair of boots standing on the cover. I held my breath. My heart began to thump unnecessarily loudly, and I expected the man to look down at any moment.

At last he moved off. Inspecting the cover again, I noticed quite a lot of rust on one side, and I hit this part hard until it began to move. It squeaked and groaned and then yielded. As I eased it up slowly, it fell on one side and caught my finger. It wasn't my day. This was a ridiculous situation—a respected scientist from a distinguished university with his head poking out of a manhole cover in the middle of the multi-launching pad, with security men running around like rabbits.

Betelgeuse's rocket stood motionless about a hundred yards away. The whole scene looked rather macabre with flashes of flame leaping round.

I eased myself out of the hole and ran towards the foreign ship. I listened intently for running feet but there weren't any. Just the thundering sound of a rocket going up.

Near Betelgeuse's ship a rather nasty thought struck me. What happens if the airlock doors aren't open? It was impossible to see whether they were open or not until I was right up against the craft. They weren't. Looking back over my shoulder I could see a small security vehicle approaching at high speed. They must have a bell or something, I thought to myself, searching for some way of getting in. To my surprise, the doors swung apart. Inside I made for the lift door, which opened as soon as the outer doors had closed. A great feeling of relief and hysteria came over me, and the more I tried to control the situation the worse it became and I started to laugh.

'You have a strange way of visiting us,' said Alcyone, standing by the lift as the door into the main cabin opened.

'Why?' I said, laughing.

Betelgeuse, who was over at the far side of the cabin also started to laugh. 'You looked so funny,' he said. 'Suddenly appearing from a hole in the ground and running towards us.'

'It felt funny,' I said, with tears beginning to come into my eyes.

131

'You're both stupid,' Alcyone said crossly.

'Alcyone,' I said. 'It is only an outlet for emotion and tension.'

'Maybe so, but what about that?' she said, pointing at the slumped figure of Betelgeuse. He lifted his head and I thought he looked tired and rather sad.

'You are right,' he said soberly. 'It is a wonderful relief for tension and frustration.'

I walked over to where he now sat. 'What do you think?' I said, looking over his shoulder at the small TV monitor. The security car was parked below us and they seemed to be having difficulty in opening the airlock doors. Then Betelgeuse manually moved the outside camera to take in more of the area. Another ship fired up and left the launching area in a cloud of sparks.

I said, 'They don't look any different from the ships that have been going up for years.'

'They're not any different except for more advanced radar and weapons,' Alcyone said, coming to join us.

'But why?' I said to myself.

'They don't believe the seriousness of the enemy.'

'What about your forces?' I asked Betelgeuse.

'I have had them withdrawn deep into space out of the way of what will happen.'

'Ours are going to be massacred.'

'They are being. There's a big panic on. The first ships have already been picked off by the Essan advanced force. It would also appear that there's a very big concentration of ships somewhere on the far side of the sun.'

'Then . . .' I was so flabbergasted at the thought of what the world governments were up to, I had to sit down. I lost no more time. 'Betelgeuse, there is only one way of getting on equal terms with the enemy.'

'How do you mean?' Alcyone asked anxiously.

'Well, let's face it, any creature that can move large quantities of gas around at great speed, has an advantage over you as well as us here on Earth. But we have one ally more powerful than the enemy,' I said enthusiastically.

'Impossible,' Betelgeuse said.

'No, the Sun, our Sun.'

'The Sun! How can it help?' asked Alcyone.

'Increase the flare activity enormously,' I said, warming to my thoughts. 'Cause it to emit a tremendous blast of high-speed particles—cosmic rays really—which would completely cook any living matter inside the solar system.'

'A very interesting idea, but it would seem to be impractical,' Betelgeuse said.

'No, look, it's very well known the activity going on, on the Sun's surface—flares, sunspots and so on—comes from the boiling motion of gas just below the skin.'

Both Alcyone and Betelgeuse nodded.

'The next point is the cause of the boiling motion,' I said.

'Heat from below,' Alcyone said.

'Yes. If there was no heat from below there would

133

be no boiling—naturally. But also, if the extreme surface skin of the Sun were different—if it contained a much higher concentration of metal atoms—there wouldn't be any boiling either. O.K.?' I said, even more enthusiastic with the idea. 'Well, I want to increase the concentration of metals in that surface skin—to stop the need for the boiling. The idea being that all the energy of motion existing at the moment would suddenly be released in an explosion—of flares and cosmic rays.'

'It is a rather strange theory,' said Betelgeuse.

'You see, we could drop a load of metals at the surface. I think it would trigger off a big outburst.'

'Any particular metal?' asked Alcyone.

'I think it would be best to use the lightest one—lithium—so that we could carry more of the stuff. I want a sort of solar lithium bomb. I know it sounds a crazy idea, but it's just possible it might work.'

'You need our help?' Betelgeuse said.

'Yes,' I said rather shyly after my outburst. 'It isn't easy to drop anything directly into the Sun; if you're the slightest bit off target, your bomb will whip into orbit around the Sun instead of falling to its surface.'

'Yes. You'll have to go a long way in towards the Sun, before starting off the bomb.'

'Quite. The problem with our ships is they're not well enough refrigerated for a trip far in, close to the Sun. We'd fry long before we were near enough.'

'Alcyone,' said Betelgeuse. 'Could I have the spectra of this Sun?'

Rigel and the rest of the crew appeared from the lift.

134

Alcyone dimmed the lights and a large spectrum appeared on the wall. Betelgeuse explained very quickly what I'd been saying. Rigel looked long and hard at the spectrum, and made some calculations.

'It could be the right sort of star,' Rigel said thoughtfully.

'Dwarf G 2,' said Betelgeuse.

'Dwarf G 2!' I said.

'Yes, it seems possible that your idea could work,' Rigel said with a somewhat wicked smile.

'That's wonderful,' I said.

'Dick,' Alcyone said. 'We may be able to drop your bomb, but someone will have to get the bomb, as well as convince your authorities that it will not affect Earth. Have you thought of that?'

'I don't really think the Earth will get that cooked. Our atmosphere and magnetic field should protect us.'

'Not if the cosmic rays come in with very high energies,' Betelgeuse said.

'Yes, I suppose so. The showers could come right down to ground level. But it isn't likely the energies would be that high.'

'Nevertheless, you will have to clear this with your people. We can't be responsible for cooking Earth,' Betelgeuse said with a grin.

'No, no. Of course you can't,' I said. 'I will present the idea to a friend and see what his reaction is. Then we can move from there.'

9

I left Betelgeuse's ship in high spirits. It occurred to me as the lift descended that they might think I was mad, but the idea was too good not to try.

The airlock doors opened and there stood Colonel Rhodes and Ganges. Ganges looked very angry indeed.

'Dick,' said Rhodes, standing there with his hands on his hips.

'Hello, Colonel; you weren't worried, were you?'

'Of course we were, old man. It's a bad loophole in our security system. I'd never thought of those communication tunnels,' said Colonel.

'Makes me look ruddy stupid,' said Ganges. 'If you'd come to the front gate we wouldn't have had this damned security panic,' he said, looking very upset. We all turned and walked over to the terminal buildings.

'Would you have let me through?'

'No,' he bristled.

'Is everything O.K.?' I asked Colonel.

'I think so,' he said in a whisper.

'Why didn't you tell me you wanted to come,' Colonel said in a loud voice so Ganges could hear.

I looked at him and winked. 'Impulse, I think. What's going on?'

'We've got to get all this lot off the ground as fast as possible,' Ganges answered.

'Do you know you're losing your forward ships?' I said.

'Betelgeuse told you?' Colonel said, looking hard at me.

'Was there anything wrong in that?' I asked.

'Of course there was. He's just laughing at our vain attempts to have a go at these creatures. It makes me livid; he's withdrawn all his fleet into deep space, leaving us wide open,' Ganges said.

'Wouldn't you?' I said, defending Betelgeuse.

'How do you mean?'

'Well, did you or your commanders inform him of what had been decided?'

'I've no idea,' said Ganges.

'He thinks you're mad. Wasting your lives in a fruitless attempt. I can see his point. Why should he join our foolishness; he went through all that when the galactic war started.'

'What the hell were we expected to do? Sit and think about the problem until they fry us a lovely golden brown? You scientists are all the same,' Ganges said.

'Nobody consulted me,' I said turning to Colonel.

'Why should we, you'd only sit and think,' Ganges said angrily.

'Maybe, but if the politicians and military had bothered to use their brains, there does happen to be another solution to the immediate problem,' I retaliated.

'I suppose that means you've got some hare-brained

138

scheme to save the world,' Ganges said sarcastically.

'No, let's say an idea that might save the present situation, not necessarily a permanent solution.'

'What did the great white chief say?' Colonel said, indicating Betelgeuse's ship.

'He's willing to put his life and ship in danger to see if it will work.'

We walked on in silence into the building. The place was in a turmoil. Crews getting instructions—illuminated maps flashing numbers and the constant noise from the TV monitors giving the latest world information on how the operation was going.

Rhodes wended his way through all these bodies and equipment until he reached an office. I closed the door behind us, and the silence was almost beautiful. Ganges and I sat down and Colonel went behind his desk and pressed some buttons.

'Andy, have you any idea where the Chief is?' Colonel said.

'He's on his way to W.H.Q., sir,' came the voice.

'Well, that's given us a break. Ganges, can we give Dick a pass?'

Ganges thought for a moment and then nodded. 'It'll save wear and tear on the tunnels.'

'Ganges,' I blurted out. 'You must have known about the tunnels. It was a bit too easy.'

'Hrrmph,' snorted Ganges. 'Carry out orders as best I can—don't expect crackpots to creep through tunnels to have a chat with friends.'

'I had to see Betelgeuse—I'm really on to something.'

'Yes, so Sir John thought,' drawled Ganges. 'Too long through usual channels—so use tunnels.'

'Ganges, you're a damned old fraud!"

'Wish Sir John was as complimentary,' he chortled. 'Boffins!'

'Andy, can you bring me a security pass?' Colonel said into his intercom and closed the channel. We waited in a suspended silence until the pass had been delivered.

'Here you are, Dick. Next time let us know,' said Ganges with a grin, signing the card and handing it to me.

'Well, what is this idea?' Colonel said.

'It's very simple really. The enemy will be proceeding farther into our solar system. Now we don't have much of a chance with our weapons, even a Quark torpedo, in out-shooting them. The idea came to me, we could use the Sun as a sort of radiation bomb,' I said, looking at the two grim-faced men.

'What sort of radiation bomb?'

'I was thinking of dropping a load of lithium on to the Sun's surface.' Briefly I explained the whole idea.

'Lithium bomb, eh? Quite ingenious. Fry the enemy,' Ganges said unwinding his dejected body and getting up.

'You think it has possibilities?' Colonel said to both of us.

'Hm. Problem is—who's going to drop it?—got a charley?'

'We can't,' said Colonel, 'our ships haven't got the gear.'

'Betelgeuse has agreed to take it,' I said.

'Couldn't be better—good judge of a man—he'll do!' Ganges' shorthand hid a mind few guessed at. 'What about you?'

'Certainly. If it was thought necessary.'

'Work out what you'd need—I'll put military wheels in motion,' Ganges said, opening the door. 'Good idea, very good,' he said and closed the door behind him.

Colonel looked at me, and we both laughed.

'A strange man,' I said.

'Certainly, but now he's got the bit between his teeth you're set.'

'Do you really think he can do anything? He's always rubbed me up the wrong way.'

'Certainly. As you gather, he's got a wonderful ability for cutting through all the red tape, when it suits his purpose.'

There was a loud knock at the door.

'Come in,' Colonel said abruptly.

'Good evening, Colonel Rhodes,' said one of the police officers coming into the room.

'Good evening, officer. What can I do for you?'

'We're looking for a man who might have entered the launching pad area,' said the policeman.

'Really! How do we know?' Rhodes said, looking sideways at me.

'Well, we had a report from Cambridge that someone stole a canoe and a hover speed boat. When we were looking round, we found the hover boat on the river, near one of the radar aerials.'

'I see,' said Colonel. 'Well, I haven't heard anything, but just a moment.' He flicked a switch.

'Colonel Ganges, please.'

'Ganges here,' came the reply after a moment.

'Rhodes here. Have you heard anything about someone possibly entering the launching area illegally?'

'Not a word, old man, not a word.'

'I'm sorry to bother you,' said the policeman.

'That's quite all right. If I do hear anything I'll let you know.'

The policeman backed out of the room.

'Why on earth . . . ?'

'Dick, I don't approve of what you did, but if there is anything in your lithium bomb idea, we'd have to wait weeks for clearance to work on the project. Do you want to work here or at home?'

'I'll work at home, thanks. I don't want your people breathing down my neck.'

'O.K.' Colonel smiled. 'I'll arrange transport.'

It felt pleasant to be home. It made me smile to think of Ganges' being an accessory to my boat stealing and entering a military establishment without permission. After making a cup of tea, I searched for a book I'd had from the University Library, on sun flares. Inside the cover it read: "This book must *not* be removed from the Library.' I began to wonder how long I'd had the blessed thing, not that this was important at the moment. Though sun flares were.

The calculations were relatively simple, and soon I knew the quantity of lithium required. For some reason the result didn't make me feel happy or jubilant, instead it made me realize the heavy responsibility. This was natural, but it was also rather disturbing. Would the idea work? It had all the possibilities but I couldn't guarantee it would. I would have given anything for someone to come along and share the risk.

'And I believe I'm right,' I said out loud to the unlistening world.

Colonel was looking lined and tired when I got through on the phone.

'Any luck, Dick?' said Colonel.

'You look all in.'

'So would you. We have just finished shoving up thousands of craft, only to be told that they're all to be brought back.'

'You poor fellow,' I laughed, instantly feeling more cheerful. 'Well, now you can get your teeth into my lithium bomb. You'll need in the order of four hundred tons of lithium.'

'What! four hundred tons!' cried Colonel in despair.

I nodded.

'How do you think we're going to store the stuff in the direct heat of the Sun?'

'The only thing I can think of is to pack the stuff in high temperature oil, all installed in a refrigerated vacuum.'

Colonel looked horrified at the thought. 'Let me get my people to look into the problem. Betelgeuse is giving us one of his torpedoes, but modified to travel as fast as possible from roughly the orbit of Mercury to the Sun.'

'That sounds fine. By the way, have you had any political reaction?' I asked.

'I told you Ganges could cut red tape. That's why we're getting the order for total withdrawal from space. By the way, you've cooked your own goose, as it were. Betelgeuse says that he wants you to go with the bomb.'

'You mean to the Sun?'

'Yes. He wants you along with him and the powers that be have agreed.'

'Thanks. Let me know the time of Operation Cremation.'

I didn't catch Colonel's funny remark as I flicked the switch, so all I saw was his laughing face fade off the screen. Having forgotten to ask him how long it would be before they might be ready, I was in a quandary as to whether I should get some sleep or pack.

Instead of worrying I looked through the calculations, reworking and reworking the problem. The answer kept coming out the same every time, which didn't really improve my state of mind. I put the sheet of paper on one side and closed my eyes.

The fear of being trapped in space became more vivid. My suspicious mind began to work along the lines that, if Alcyone wanted her way, it would be very easy. Betelgeuse could agree to take the bomb, but he might not be sold on my idea, so she says we'll take Warboys along, if the idea works they'd bring me home, if not, onward far into space. You conceited old fraud, I thought.

Sleep must have eventually overtaken me, for I woke with a start. Shivering, I went to the kitchenette. It was nearly 6.10, and the wall thermometer showed $21°$ centigrade, so I wasn't shivering through cold.

The water in the shower was very hot and I slowly shook off the horrible sleepy feeling. Turning off the water, I switched the hot air drier on, then I put on clean clothes. It suddenly struck me why I'd had the shivering fit. I had got very wet crawling along the communications tunnel and had forgotten all about it. I probably had a slight temperature. The clean clothes felt wonderful, as did the cup of coffee I made. The doorbell rang. Funny, I thought, who'd be calling at this hour? I took another sip of coffee and then went to the door.

'Sorry to disturb you,' said Alcyone, standing there.

'Hello, you're up and about very early,' I said, opening the door wider to allow her in.

'Dick, everything is ready now.'

'So you've come to fetch me?' I said guardedly.

'No, I've come to have a word with you,' Alcyone said, sitting down. 'Do you realize what could happen to the Earth when the bomb is dropped?'

'Certainly, I have a fairly good idea.'

'I was talking to Colonel Rhodes and apparently none

of the politicians or military have thought out the consequences.'

'So they're willing to take a risk?' I said.

'Risk very high energy particles?'

'I know. At worst a few people will lose their lives. Surely that is better than killing everyone?'

Alcyone smiled and nodded. 'I suppose so.'

'Anyway, why does Betelgeuse want me along?'

'He reasons that, if he's going to risk his life, then you can jolly well risk yours,' Alcyone said with a laugh.

I had to smile as well, after what I had originally thought.

'Would you like a cup of something?'

'No, it's time we were leaving,' Alcyone said.

'But I thought you said you hadn't come to fetch me?' I said in surprise.

'I haven't come, it is Colonel Rhodes who has come. I came so I could ask you my question.'

I must have looked a little confused.

'I'm not going,' she said finally. 'You and Betelgeuse are going by yourselves.'

'Can the two of us control the ship?'

'Certainly. One person could operate it.'

'So you and the rest of the crew are staying here?' I stopped speaking. The thought struck me that perhaps Betelgeuse reckoned that we wouldn't get out of the blast from the Sun in time.

Alcyone walked with me down to where Colonel was parked. She gave me a big kiss and then moved back.

'Come on, Dick, we haven't all morning.'

'Hm,' I said, climbing into the helicopter.

The journey was accomplished in a thoughtful silence. The morning mists were just clearing off the fields as we flew over them. Then I could see the space drome. This time it was crammed with space craft. Colonel manœuvred the helicopter into a space near Betelgeuse's ship. At the airlock door, Colonel took hold of my hand and shook it hard.

'Good luck,' he said with a tremor in his voice.

'Thanks. Will you do me a favour?'

'Certainly,' Colonel said, still holding my hand.

'When we've gone, will you make sure that Alcyone is all right?'

'Of course. I think she'll be staying with Sir John Fielding.'

'That's good,' I said, climbing into the airlock. To my surprise all Betelgeuse's crew were standing there.

'By God, you're all going to get a shock when we come back.'

Rigel smiled. 'That's a good way to think.'

I shook hands with them and went up in the lift. Ganges and Betelgeuse were standing talking.

'Hello, Dick. Not too early I hope,' Ganges beamed.

'Far too early,' I replied.

'Well, you'll be able to catch up a whole day's sleep before you start getting too hot.'

'Thanks. Are we all set?' I said, looking at Betelgeuse, who didn't look at all unhappy; in fact he had a wicked twinkle in his eyes.

'Well, I'll leave you to it,' Ganges said, getting into the lift.

'Dick, how are you under acceleration?'

'Not too good.'

'Well, we've put a couple of bunks in. Take your pick,' Betelgeuse said.

I went over to the bunks and lay down on one. Betelgeuse came and settled in on the other. With him he brought a portable control panel, which struck me as far more sensible than the fixed ones we used.

'All doors closed,' Betelgeuse said.

'Pad clear and ready for take off,' came the controller's voice over the radio intercom.

'Betelgeuse,' came Colonel's voice. 'We've a report that there are ships in the orbit of Jupiter. They are not moving.'

'Serious?' I asked.

'Are they on the far side of the Sun?' Betelgeuse asked.

'At present, yes,' Colonel's reply crackled.

'Ready, Dick?' Betelgeuse asked.

I nodded and my stomach felt very strange. The craft began to accelerate. The pressure wasn't quite what I expected. In our own ships, by now it would be highly uncomfortable. Looking at Betelgeuse, I began to understand. He had the ship at about quarter throttle.

'When does it get bad?' I asked.

'You're through the worst. At each stage, as we become accustomed to the acceleration, I'll open it up a little more, until we are going as fast as we can manage.' He climbed off his bunk and went off out of my sight. If he can do it I can, I thought, swinging my legs off the bunk. It didn't do me much good, as I was walking round on my knees. Betelgeuse laughed and helped me back. He returned to his bunk and handed me something to drink.

'It'll make you sleep for a while,' he said.

'How long?' I asked, not wanting to miss anything.

'At most a couple of hours, long enough to get used to the acceleration without mental tension.'

'Fine,' I said, draining the container. Nothing seemed to happen.

The faint buzz woke me up. Betelgeuse had a pair of earphones on and in front of him was a monitor. I manœuvred myself on to an elbow to get a look. To my amazement, he was watching a Western film. He looked my way for a moment, smiled, and turned back to his viewing. Climbing off my bunk I found that I could stand without any problem. Time had flown. According to my watch, I must have been asleep for over eight hours. The monitor for the outside cameras was on. I searched the dark space outside for something which I might recognize. By now we should have been able to see Venus quite well.

Betelgeuse took one of his earphones off. 'We should be inside the orbit of Venus.'

I looked again, but there was nothing except darkness. He leaned forward and pushed a button. 'Is that better?'

I manœuvred the cameras and then I found the

planet. It almost filled the screen, so we must be getting very close. I went on moving the cameras until I found what I was really looking for, a small spot of light which represented the Earth. Betelgeuse had gone back to his film, but before doing that he'd put up a chart of our course and the relative positions of the planets Mercury and Venus. Being a scientist, not a military tactician, it took me a few minutes to work out the logic of his plan.

The ship had been plotted so as to pass very close to Venus on its darkened side. From there we would make our way to Mercury since Mercury was at the present nearly on the far side of the Sun in its orbiting. The plot went just a little farther beyond the Sun, and stopped.

Suddenly the monitor lit up like the 4th of July. I looked at the brilliant light and realized we were out of the shadow of Venus. At that moment the radar screen became very active. It showed the Sun as a huge blob to the left of the screen. Mercury was situated in the middle. As well as these there was a tiny blob of light floating around the right of the screen. I watched it for a moment and then took a pad and started calculating. It was obviously much larger than one space craft, but it could be a block of them flying in close formation. I looked at the chart and found the object was just on the outside of Mercury's orbit, which would probably make it an asteroid.

'You don't think I'd be that stupid?' Betelgeuse said from behind me.

'How do you mean?'

'I'm going to give myself a chance to get into the shadow of something when this bomb goes off. One of my fleet reported an asteroid close to Mercury, so if we discharge the bomb from the far side of Mercury we have a fifty/fifty chance of getting into the shelter of this asteroid.'

'Good idea. One thing I don't like about your plan is that we are open to the enemy's radar once we move out of Mercury's shelter,' I said.

'I agree, but it is good. If they see us they will follow but they won't have time to get near enough before the bomb goes off.'

'And catches them right in the middle.'

'That's right. It should give them quite a surprise,' Betelgeuse said with a laugh.

'Let's hope so!'

'We'll be able to follow the bomb on the radar until it gets into the Sun's corona; by then I hope we're in sight of safety,' Betelgeuse said, still grinning.

I walked round the cabin trying to work out the possibilities of being safe, but without much success.

'Listen to this,' said Betelgeuse. The intercom crackled but apart from this everything was silent.

'I don't understand,' I said.

'It is strange that the Yela have stopped communicating amongst themselves.'

'Maybe they're listening.'

'You're right, waiting for our next move.'

'Do you think they know?' I asked.

'It is difficult to know what they are doing, or what they know; remember nobody has ever seen them, or at least if anyone has they've never lived to tell the tale.'

'But do you think they know where we are now?'

'Not unless they've got some radar outposts near the Earth. My ships got rid of most of these outriders and I didn't see any on the way out.'

Betelgeuse got up off the bunk and moved over to the radar screen. We looked together. The glaring white blob of the Sun was now growing impossibly bright.

To one side I could make out the asteroid, which seemed to have a magnetic pull to my eyes.

'You know, I suddenly feel rather thirsty,' I said.

'If you go to the cabin below, you will find most of your Earth drinks and the water in the pipe should be boiling. There are also space rations of Earth food.'

'Splendid,' I said, moving over to the lift.

'I suggest you take the space rations rather than solid foods, it will help your stomach and you won't feel sick.'

'Don't worry, the thought of pushing down solid food doesn't really appeal,' I said, holding my stomach and laughing.

The galley, as I suppose some people call it, was very simple. A hot water pipe with a pressure gauge, but no washing bowl or anything. Below a working top were some deep freezers. In one of them I found the coffee and made myself a drink. There didn't appear to be any milk tablets so I drank it black. The space rations were all in boxes with numbers on them. Not knowing what the numbers stood for I took one from each of several boxes and swallowed them with the coffee. My stomach felt empty, but the coffee worked wonders.

Back up in the cabin, I found Betelgeuse watching the radar scope with immense interest.

'We're being followed!' Betelgeuse said with amusement.

'What!' The idea was ridiculous.

'I was just testing the radar aerial at the rear of the ship to see that it was opening and closing, when I picked this up.'

There was nothing to be seen at first as the large mass of Venus behind us was extremely big, but then I noticed a small dot crossing the surface of the planet. 'How near is it?'

'About four to five hours and travelling at about the same speed.'

'It isn't one of yours, is it?'

'No, I tested it with our recognition signal, but there was no reply. I also tried your Earth distress signal just in case, but no response.'

I had to raise my hat to the imagination of this stranger from space; he had the cunning of a fox. I'd never have thought of using our mayday signal for a recognition count.

'What do you think?' Betelgeuse said, working the punch operator. 'We haven't time to stop and find out who it is behind us. I have a suspicion whoever it is is trying to slow us down, so we'll leave a torpedo here. I'll leave it with a radio message, so that as the ship passes in about four hours it will get a message asking its origin. If there is no reply then the torpedo will home in, and bang.'

Betelgeuse lay down to have a nap. The Western he had been watching had looked interesting, so I checked through the index of films available and flicked the switch. Time passed in a hot haze of desert and gun shots.

There was a buzz from somewhere. Betelgeuse woke up and went over to the radar screen.

'Dick,' he called. 'Our tail has caught up with the torpedo.'

The screen showed the tiny follower some four hours behind. Then there was a brilliant little flash.

'Well, he wasn't very friendly, was he,' said Betelgeuse.

'Certainly not.' I looked hard, but there weren't any more ships. Betelgeuse was now scanning with the radio equipment. Instead of the quiet we'd had earlier during the journey, space was now full of sounds.

'It was our enemy.'

'The Yela?' I said.

Betelgeuse smiled and nodded.

'Have you noticed anything?' I said.

'You mean the heat,' Betelgeuse said, looking at me.

'Is that what's making me feel thirsty?'

Betelgeuse nodded. 'It's nearly 800° centigrade, outside.'

'Whew! Hot enough to melt lead. We must be well

inside the orbit of Mercury,' I said. 'How much heat can the outside shell stand?'

'I don't think it will be the ship that suffers first, it will be us. The refrigeration plant is going at full power. I've dried the atmosphere, so we can stand up to around 80° centigrade.'

'What happens then?'

'You will see in a moment,' Betelgeuse handed me a thermometer. It read 62° centigrade.

The radar monitor was now filled with the Sun, its huge surface boiling and bubbling away.

'We'll put it in around there,' I said, pointing to a flare point in the surface. Betelgeuse made some adjustments to the sighting mechanism. My legs were beginning to feel rubbery. The temperature was now 70.90° centigrade.

We sweated quietly, neither of us moving more than was necessary.

'Hullo there, are you O.K.? Over,' came an enquiry in a very polite English voice.

'Hullo, Earth H.Q. We're having a sauna bath. Have you a message for us?' Betelgeuse asked.

'The Yela force seems to be on the move. We got a report from one of your people who was moving fast out of the solar system.'

'Don't blame them,' said Betelgeuse. 'We shall make for cover as soon as we have dropped the bomb.' He glanced at the clock in front of him. 'In about two minutes fifty seconds now.'

'It's time to get our heads down,' Betelgeuse said,

walking unsteadily over to the bunks, and I followed. He strapped himself down, so I did too; and we stared at the monitor.

Suddenly in front of us was the vast Sun. The target area was dead in centre; the bomb was locked on course.

'You ready?' Betelgeuse said calmly. I nodded, with the sinking feeling of a visit to the dentist. 'Here we go.'

'Bomb away.' I clung to the side of my bunk.

The ship started to spin end over end. One minute the Sun was on the screen, the next it wasn't. Then she suddenly steadied up and we were on our way back to safety as fast as the ship could go.

'I've tuned the radio into Earth's H.Q., who will be able to give us details of any events that we cannot see.'

I felt terrible; the ship just went on accelerating. She must be incredibly powerful, I thought, since the main cabin was also the acceleration cabin. Even taking off from Earth hadn't been as bad as this. We had nearly an hour to go to the safety of the asteroid.

'Well, we're on course,' Betelgeuse said after about ten minutes. 'What are you thinking?' he asked me.

'Well,' I said, looking at the picture of the Sun's surface. 'It looks just about the most terrible thing I've ever seen, even without an explosion. Look at the activity. Imagine what will happen if the whole thing explodes.'

'If it does, there'll be something wrong with your calculations.' Betelgeuse laughed.

'Yes, and no more worries about Earth, Betelgeuse, Warboys or the Yela.'

The weird musical sound was now quite loud, persistent and irritating as well as frightening.

'Hello, Sac Peak, H.Q. speaking. Can you say whether solar activity is higher than anything previously experienced?' we heard the English voice from World H.Q.

'Activity is very high, but not outside previous experience. Fifteen minutes ago it looked as if something unusual was happening. If the intensity of H alpha had gone on increasing, we'd have had the father and mother of all flares. But for the last ten minutes the intensity has been falling off slowly.'

'It looks as though it was a miss,' I said.

'I was on target.'

'Not your shooting, it was the theory behind the idea I was referring to.'

'Look at that!' Betelgeuse suddenly said, sitting up.

'What?'

'Here, watch the patch by the sunspots near the east limb. It's brightening very quickly.'

'It's only brightening along the usual sort of thread. What I want is the whole surface to go up,' I said damply.

The path of the brightness was spreading slowly like a snake across a small part of the surface. Then suddenly the whole thread began to widen at an incredible speed.

'How far are we from the asteroid?' I asked.

'Too far,' Betelgeuse said, punching some new instructions. 'We'll change course and head right into the sheltered side of Mercury. That should take us twenty minutes.'

'Twenty minutes! . . . Look it's going right round the east limb.'

'Well, you'll be glad to know that your calculations look right now,' Betelgeuse said, wiping the sweat from his forehead.

'Maybe, but I wish I had more knowledge of this type of thing.'

'The whole damn thing's going up,' Betelgeuse said.

'It's going to boil,' I said jubilantly.

'Yes, and we're going to get cooked alive along with everything else.'

'How long?' I said.

'No time at all. Those particles are travelling at nearly the speed of light.'

'Certainly, but there's just a chance, with it being towards the east of the Sun. There's usually a longer delay between the particles and light when it's on that side.'

'Of course. The magnetic field, but that'll be shot to pieces.'

'Normally, yes. But that boiling must be bringing up a lot of new magnetic field from below. It may hold back the particles for a few moments.'

'Maybe,' Betelgeuse said, watching the instruments in front of him.

'By God. It's fantastic. It looks as if the whole Sun is blowing up!'

10

Suddenly the great fireball vanished from the screen.

I looked at Betelgeuse. He sat punching out another message for the computer system, the sweat running off his hands on to the punch keys.

'Hello, Warboys. Ganges. Over,' came the crackling voice over the intercom.

'Warboys here. How's everything down there? Over,' I said.

'Sun's just given off the biggest ruddy flare in history. Are you sheltered? Over.'

'Reasonably, I think.' Betelgeuse was pointing to something on the control panel. I went over to look at the panel. The outside radiation counters were going mad, and the inside counter was climbing up to human limit.

'The radiation out here is fantastic. Over.'

'Anything you want? Over,' said Ganges.

'Yes,' said Betelgeuse. 'As soon as the flare intensity decreases let us know.'

'O.K. Over and out,' said Ganges.

My eyes were now fixed on the radiation counters. The indoor counter was rising slowly but surely.

'Is there any cure for an overdose of radiation?' I asked Betelgeuse.

He smiled. 'Not here. The only way we can counteract extensive burning is to replace the burnt tissue. Unfortunately our medical unit is too far away to be able to help us if we are exposed to too big a dose.'

'That's cheerful. I'd hate to be out there in the full impact of this bombardment.'

An explosion rocked the ship. Betelgeuse somehow managed to remain standing as I went down on my shoulder with a bang.

'Essans,' he yelled.

I got up, only to be thrown back on my face, from the fierce acceleration coupled with another explosion. The Sun suddenly appeared on the tele-cine, then it vanished.

'Sorry, we've got to outmanœuvre them,' Betelgeuse shouted.

'How many are there?' I asked.

'Three, I think.'

Again the Sun appeared. I waited until everything seemed to be going smoothly, then got up. The radar antenna was homed on the three ships.

'What are they waiting for?'

'They are trying to work out what frequencies we are jamming. The torpedoes can be thrown off course by jamming the operation frequencies.'

'You mean before you commence battle, you compute all the possible combinations?'

'Sometimes. I find it simplest to get close in on the

enemy and pick up the jamming frequencies, then it's just a question of who has the fastest electronics.'

'Just like playing a vast game of chess.'

'Yes, I suppose so, but you see our problem is how to solve the frequencies for one ship and hit it, meantime trying to baffle them so as not to get hit.'

'In that case how did you manage to bag the ship that was shadowing us?'

'When you've a situation like that it's easy. You set the homing devices to work so that if one frequency is jammed it moves over to the next. Each time it hits an unjammed one it moves in until cut off. Sooner or later it will hit its target because the enemy hasn't enough time to compute your next frequency. You can understand the destruction could take many hours.'

'Why did the Essans do that just now?'

'They're not fighters. They fire first and then think out the tactics after they've lost,' Betelgeuse said in disgust.

I looked at the radiation counters. Inside the ship was now close to the danger limit. Betelgeuse was looking serious. He came over, checked the radiation counter and then the radar screen.

'Come with me,' he said, getting into the lift. We went down to the crew's quarters. In a large wall cupboard were the space suits I'd seen Betelgeuse and his crew wearing originally. He rummaged around and pulled out two dull grey suits. They looked very heavy and he could barely pull them from the cupboard.

'What on earth are those?' I asked.

161

'Lead anti-radiation suits.'

'Surely it's not going to help much now,' I said, wondering what the actual physical pain of radiation would be.

'Oh, I think you'll find it will help quite a lot. Here,' he said. 'Hang on to that.'

I took hold of the suit. Betelgeuse went over to a punch machine. If I'd known what was going on I'd have held on to the lead suit with more conviction.

Suddenly I became weightless and floated to the ceiling. Betelgeuse roared with laughter and began to climb into his suit. Once in the suit he threw up a small piece of lifeline and pulled me down.

'Very funny,' I said.

'You put your suit on,' Betelgeuse said, taking one of my legs and helping it into the suit. Once on, although action was a little stagy, my feet remained on the ground. A helmet was produced and this was fitted very carefully.

'How's that?' came Betelgeuse's voice through the headphones.

'Damned hot.'

'We'll see what we can do about that.'

We arrived back in the main cabin. Betelgeuse hurried over to the radar screen. There were only two ships left. He set the scanner going and there was the third ship, manœuvring in behind us.

'Time to move,' he said, pressing a lever on the control box. A panel slid open revealing hoses, all coiled up like the old-fashioned fire hoses. He uncoiled one and attached it to my waistband. Slowly the heat inside the suit began to decrease.

'What is it?'

'A form of air conditioning. Pure air.'

That's a relief, I thought to myself. He handed me a second hose and I plugged it in.

'My plan of action is very simple. With these suits we should be able to go out into very high radiation values without too many bad results. So we'll make a run for home, and on the way we'll drop presents for our friends.'

'Yes, but we might get cooked to pieces.'

'True,' said Betelgeuse. 'But I'd prefer to risk that rather than a few more enemy space ships turning up.'

'Oh, I agree, but won't the high energy particles damage the ship?'

'They certainly might, but once we're bound for Earth, we won't have any problems until inside the gravitational pull of your planet.'

'Fine. Let's go,' I said, taking my position on my bunk. Betelgeuse fired the ship.

For the next few hours I watched the radiation levels and Betelgeuse worked out the positions to drop the torpedoes. The air conditioning inside my suit was marvellous and in fact I felt more nimble and raring to go than I had done for a long time.

'We've gained a little on our friends. I've laid them a little surprise.'

I looked at Betelgeuse. He smiled.

'Just on the off chance that one or two of them are

travelling on automatic pilot, I've put a torpedo in each of their paths. If that doesn't work, they'll revert back to hunting.'

I smiled. There was a certain amount of one-upmanship which amused me. I felt that since my 'bomb' idea, Betelgeuse had been trying to prove, in a nice way, that he was just as good as I was.

Betelgeuse pushed the button that released the torpedoes and smiled at me, almost reading my thoughts, I felt, so I smiled back.

'Warboys, what on earth's going on? Over,' came Ganges' voice.

'Dick, this is Colonel Rhodes. We are getting a little worried by the solar storm, over.'

I looked at Betelgeuse. He returned the look and then winked.

'Hello, Colonel. What kind of problem's worrying you? Over,' I said, while Betelgeuse smiled away.

'What do you mean?' said Rhodes. 'Great tongues of radiation are coming through the atmosphere. We've already had an outbreak of fire in London through this phenomenon. Over.'

'Well, as long as the bulk of the population stay put, it should be over inside forty-eight hours,' I said.

'Look, Warboys,' came Ganges' voice. 'We're not worried, it's the damned politicians who are getting upset and they're pressuring the military for a suitable reply to the situation.'

'It's all over up here, and it shouldn't get very much worse.' Betelgeuse shook his head in approval and

164

pointed to the radiation counters. I walked over to the counters. They hadn't gone up and appeared to be fairly steady. 'I've just looked at the radiation count and it's now holding steady. Over.'

'I hope so,' Ganges' voice said.

Then Rhodes came on the air again. 'I have a report that there are four ships on their way towards Earth. Over.'

'Well, don't worry,' I laughed. 'One of them is our ship, the other three are Essans which will be disposed of in a short period of time. Over.'

'What the hell are you doing in the storm? Over.'

'Sunbathing.' Betelgeuse chuckled.

'What was that, Dick?' came Rhodes' voice.

'Sunbathing. Over.'

The silence from Earth made me grin, as one could imagine them wondering what was going on.

'There goes one,' said Betelgeuse.

On the radar screen there were two blobs and another small cluster that for a moment looked like an illuminated dust cloud, then nothing. A small weight of worry was lifted off our minds. Apart from the light-headed feeling I now had, the biggest question was, had my idea really worked. It would be difficult to take account of the number of ships in the immediate area of the solar system at the time of the explosion. Obviously the Essans had at present escaped; how many more, I wondered, were momentarily unaffected by the heat rays.

'How quiet are the Yela?' I asked.

'It's very difficult to tell. They keep coming on and

then going off the air,' said Betelgeuse. 'As soon as the area is relatively clear of cosmic radiation I'll get a scout group in to have a look round.'

'I'll ask our people to help as well,' I said, feeling that Betelgeuse might have risked enough.

'I think my people will be able to do the job more quickly, and they can also get closer to the Sun.'

'Calling Warboys—Betelgeuse. Calling Warboys—Betelgeuse,' came Rhodes' voice.

'Warboys here,' I said.

'Calling Warboys—Betelgeuse. Calling Warboys—Betelgeuse.' The message was repeated and repeated. Betelgeuse began to work frantically with the punch operating machine. Eventually the solution came back through the print out.

'There appears to be some form of short in the output transmitter circuit and the aerial seems to be bent,' Betelgeuse said, moving towards the lift.

'Can I help?'

'You might have to. I'm not really an electrician.'

The lift descended to a point just below the crew's quarters. This let us out into the heart of the ship. It was incredibly neat and tidy. The main computer and storage lay in one big block with the subsidiary machinery, such as engines, compressors, radio, radar, air conditioning, recirculation and all other little secrets Betelgeuse had up his sleeve.

Pulling the cover of one of the subsidiary boxes, he exposed black sooty patches on the circuit cards.

'Do you fuse these systems?'

166

'Yes, on the more delicate devices such as the steering gear, but I'm not sure what Rigel and his fellows do with this lot down here,' Betelgeuse said, looking rather airily at the problem.

'Have you got any testing equipment?'

Betelgeuse looked round for a moment and then moved to a small door. He went through and I followed, more out of curiosity than anything. The room was full of laboratory equipment. In fact, I was so taken aback that I said: 'Heavens.' Betelgeuse looked at me.

'You thought we might do things with magic?' he said.

'No, it had crossed my mind but since you have a floating hospital, I assumed you'd probably have your own floating labs and repair ships.'

'That's true, but on any sort of expedition one must carry a few of the necessary tools. What do you want?'

'A volt meter or anything that will register current.'

'That of course will be the one piece of equipment we're lacking,' laughed Betelgeuse going through some cupboards.

I thought hard; the problem of short circuit with the radio equipment might be simple, but if not, would it be worth repairing?

'How long will it be before we are back home?' I asked.

'Twenty-four hours, unless we get some form of malfunction.'

'Is it possible to pinpoint the trouble with the radio?'

'Certainly, if you give me the information.'

I went back to the radio equipment. The circuit cards made our radios look like toy transmitters. I pulled each one out and studied it for soot or burning. There seemed to be two cards that looked rather unhappy. I took them in the lab. I didn't try to repair them myself; surely Rigel would carry spares. As I thought, in one of the trays in the cupboard were a great mass of cards. Finding the ones I wanted didn't take long.

'What would you like to know?' Betelgeuse said, putting down some sort of file.

'Hm. Let's start with the aerial, then work back to the transmitter here. All I really want to know is if it is a short circuit, is it simply a positive negative connection or something serious?'

Betelgeuse nodded and got to work. The information came back at him almost immediately. While he was interpreting it, I checked the connections for the cards and then slipped them back in their positions.

'It says here that the fault runs from about two meters from the transmitter to the aerial, which is now non-existent. If that is the case, the heat we have been in has melted the aerial and the system has shorted from there in,' Betelgeuse said thoughtfully.

'What about the other equipment?' I said.

'Oh, there is no problem. There is a secondary aerial, according to that file I was reading. The thing that makes me annoyed is that, if the aerial had been pulled in at the time of the explosion, we'd have been all right.' Betelgeuse moved towards the lift.

168

'This means that all external equipment is probably damaged?'

'Yes, but everything is doubled. All circuitry and all external equipment, except torpedo carriers.'

'Then we can use the auxiliary radio equipment,' I said.

'That's what I thought, but it appears that the secondary circuit is fed along near the first, and in the case of the radio transmitter the two have gone.'

'But we can hear incoming messages.'

'Certainly; that's a different aerial.'

We returned to the main cabin. Betelgeuse went over to the radar screen. Everything seemed to be functioning properly, except that there were still two bright blobs on the screen.

'Something must have gone wrong,' I observed.

'No, not necessarily. Having seen one of their ships hit, they're probably furiously calculating the problem of trying to avoid the torpedoes.'

'Calling Betelgeuse or Warboys. Calling Betelgeuse or Warboys.' The message was repeated and repeated continuously, while we sat wondering what they wanted.

'Good, there goes another of them,' shouted Betelgeuse enthusiastically. I smiled in approval.

A sinister thought began to invade my mind. If Rhodes or Ganges hadn't heard me say that it was ourselves that were coming in towards the Earth, then we would be in for trouble. From what I'd gathered from the Military, if you didn't have a homing course, you were fired on.

'Betelgeuse, you remember when you first landed on Earth, we had to have a frequency to land on. Well, if we don't get one I presume they'll fire at us.'

Betelgeuse looked rather surprised at the thought and then threw his hands up in fake despair. 'You mean I've got to land through a hail of missiles?'

'Yes,' I said laughing. 'It's not your trip.'

The next day was spent in sleep or, rather, I slept while Betelgeuse spent most of the time working out the homing devices that could be used on the ground to air missiles. Sometimes when I half woke I could hear the punch card machine going, and then the print output machine would hammer away with its answers. It didn't seem really possible that we'd been away from Earth over three days. Neither Betelgeuse nor I had had much sleep and we were looking the worse for wear.

'There's an unidentified object coming up from the direction of Earth,' Betelgeuse said quietly.

On the forward radar screen was a flashing blob coming up fast. Even as we watched the object began to move away from our approach course. Then it just exploded.

'Strange,' I said aloud.

'Probably outside its range.'

'Hm.'

'Outside its target area.'

'Maybe, but here comes another,' I said, pointing to the small dot coming across the screen.

'Good, we'll be able to see how far we can get without being hit.'

I looked at Betelgeuse's sly smile. What could he have been doing with that computer of his? The light blob kept on coming and then it moved away and exploded. Betelgeuse began to look like a man who is about to burst out in song.

'All right?' I asked. 'What have you been doing?'

'Look, here comes another one,' Betelgeuse said enthusiastically. Again it was the same story, except that it moved off in a different direction.

'From what you were telling me about the ground to air missiles and the homing devices on the warhead torpedoes, I decided to give an idea a try.'

'And risk our lives!'

'No, I think we've had quite enough of that. Normally a missile is given the position and speed of the target and if the target is static the destruction is easy.'

'And on a moving target you give a position, a speed and the direction of travel. When the missile reaches a certain point in its travel you make it home on the vibrations or transmissions of your alien target,' I said.

'Right, so the development of a homing device would follow a sophisticated form of detecting vibrations of one sort or another. It would be very difficult to stop vibrations or radio emissions, so to avoid interception, you increase your ship's speed to outrun the missile and try to checkmate the missile by putting your computed course against it.'

171

'That doesn't answer my question of what you did to move the missiles off course and explode.'

The radar screen showed another blob coming in at us. But fortunately for us it destroyed itself.

'That shows you how far you can go if you use simple principles. I racked my brains to think how we could get back to Earth through a hail of missiles. So I used some laser equipment we have, placed it at various exit points, gave the laser a certain distance to operate over and then turned on the power. Having done that, one just passes heavy vibrations to the end of the beams and your missile hopefully homes in on it.'

'But surely the ship gives out more vibrations than your laser?'

'What I did was to pass a sound wave amplified many times down the laser beam, so that its noise overshadowed ours.'

'Marvellous, and I'll think it is wonderful when we're back on terra firma,' I said giving Betelgeuse a sly smile this time.

The last few hours before touch-down were quite interesting. The nearer to the Earth the heavier the barrage of missiles. Most of them exploded as they'd been doing before, but there were one or two that nearly made my heart stop. These came up on the radar screen, seemed to veer to one side and then would cut across the front or the back of our craft. Fortunately all missed but there was always the chance that something might happen. Betelgeuse waited tensely for a mishap.

'We're nearly down,' he said, turning on one of the external tele-cine cameras. The Earth was now covering the screen and I recognized the North American continent.

'Where are you going to put down?' I asked.

'England, of course.'

'Well, you'll have to go east or west of your present course.'

Betelgeuse looked hard at the Earth and then back at a chart. He punched the machine. 'I've given our destination as Mildenhall.'

'Good. What's the radioactivity reading?'

'Still well over the danger limit. We'll have to wait a few minutes before we know how serious it is.'

I went over to where Betelgeuse was standing. The radiation count was roughly where I remembered it. As the minutes went by the small needles flickered slightly, but didn't move.

'We'll be down in about five minutes,' Betelgeuse said.

I looked at the picture of the Earth. The screen now showed what looked like China. The picture began moving at a faster rate as we came near to the Earth. Suddenly we were over the Black Sea, something that might have been Germany and then fields, houses, animals.

'Hold tight,' Betelgeuse's voice crackled through the headpiece.

The retro rockets suddenly came in, making the cabin floor lurch up at me. My stomach was now somewhere in my mouth. Then we'd landed.

'I hope we don't have to go through that again,' Betelgeuse said, switching on some more outside cameras. We seemed to be jammed into a small space amongst what looked like the whole war fleet.

'How did you manage that?' I said in wonderment.

'A little bit of luck. The worst thing was the deceleration. The retro rockets didn't function at first and then when they did, instead of coming on to full power gradually, it all came on at once.'

I looked at the TV screen. There below us was a group of people standing in the rain. Betelgeuse opened the airlock door. A moment or two later the lift door opened and Ganges, Rhodes, Sir John Fielding and two other heavily braided figures floated from the lift upwards to the ceiling of the cabin. Betelgeuse's voice bellowed with mirth at the sight.

'The counters are just below danger level inside, but on the limit outside,' Betelgeuse said. 'I vote we get out of our armour.'

I struggled hard to get out, but I didn't make the mistake of letting go of the suit. 'Well, shall we let them down?' I smiled.

The punch machine was operated and then I felt weight return to my legs and body. Rhodes landed reasonably sedately, but the others made quite a hash of it.

'Dick, Betelgeuse, why didn't you say it was you coming in?' Rhodes said in exasperation.

'Radio malfunction,' Betelgeuse said, helping the others to their feet.

'How's everything here?' I said.

'Fine, but a little dangerous if you're out and about. It's been raining non-stop with tongues of flame darting through the clouds from time to time.'

'And the radiation level?'

'It's been constantly above danger level, but most of the population is underground somewhere.'

'Let's get back to the main building. The world's top brass will be coming to celebrate,' Sir John Fielding said.

We all got into the lift.

'Have there been any messages from my fleet?' Betelgeuse asked.

'Not yet,' Rhodes said. 'There is so much interference that messages might not be coming through.'

'My crew will repair this radio equipment and then we might be able to find out what has been happening,' Betelgeuse said, a little disgusted at the thought of no communications with his fleet.

Out in the open the rain came pouring down and the air smelled warm and damp. As we approached the main building, Betelgeuse's crew came rushing up to us. Betelgeuse moved forward to greet them. Great hugging and kissing took place. Alcyone came running over to me and gave me a huge hug and kiss.

'Welcome home, welcome home,' she said with tears in her eyes.

'Rigel,' I heard Betelgeuse say. 'The radio equipment is not working.'

'Right. I'll go and fix it,' Rigel said, motioning one of the crewmen towards the ship.

'When it's ready, let me know and then contact our fleet.'

Rigel smiled, saluted and moved off.

We all made our way out of the rain and into the building. Betelgeuse was being questioned about the evasive action he'd taken over the ground-to-air missiles. His replies were short and curt. I felt as he must. Anxious, wanting news of what had happened out there in space.

'It will not be long now,' Alcyone said, coming over.

Drinks began to appear. It struck me as rather funny. Were they celebrating our safe return, or the destruction we had wrought?

'There's a message from your ship,' said Ganges to Betelgeuse, handing over a micro-earpiece. A message was given. His face didn't alter but I thought I noticed a slight glint in his eye.

'Gentlemen,' said Betelgeuse. 'My second-in-command has signalled to say the enemy has retreated with very heavy losses.'

A cheer of relief went up, even Betelgeuse looked reasonably happy. There was a shaking of hands and the raising of glasses. I made my way over to Betelgeuse.

'I suppose you'll be on your way?' I said.

'Hm. I'm not sure about that,' he said. I realized that his smile was a front.

'What's wrong?'

'This,' he said, giving me the micro-earphone.

'For the time being you have won. But I am not defeated so easily,' the message came across in English. I listened to it for several moments. It just repeated itself. Betelgeuse took the micro-earphone out of my hand and smiled at me.

'Smile,' he said. I did and we turned to the rest of the party, who smiled back unknowing and innocent of things to come.